THE BONEHILL CURSE

Also by Jon Mayhew

Mortlock
The Demon Collector

THE BONEHILL CURSE

JON MAYHEW

BLOOMSBURY

LONDON BERLIN NEW YORK SYDNEY

Bloomsbury Publishing, London, Berlin, New York and Sydney

First published in Great Britain in May 2012 by Bloomsbury Publishing Plc
50 Bedford Square, London, WC1B 3DP

Epigraphs: traditional folk ballads, traditional proverbs,
proverbs from the Old Testament Book of Proverbs,
and based on *The Book of the Thousand Nights and One Night*

A CIP catalogue record for this book is available from the British Library

ISBN 978 1 4088 0397 4

Typeset by Hewer Text UK Ltd
Printed in Great Britain by Clays Ltd, St Ives plc, Bungay, Suffolk

www.bloomsbury.com
www.jonmayhew.co.uk

For Pete and Sue, Liz and Nick, Dave and Sandra
– Brothers and Sisters

He is a djinn, and I am just a man. But God has given me a sharp mind, so I will plot for his destruction with my wit and cunning just as he has plotted mine with his craft and perfidy.

The Fisherman and the Djinn,
The Book of the Thousand Nights and One Night

I curse you, Anthony Bonehill. The child that your wife so fervently wished for will kill its father. Your own kin will wish you dead.

Zaakiel

Part the First

Rookery Heights Academy for Young Ladies, 1868

PRIDE GOES BEFORE DESTRUCTION, AND A HAUGHTY SPIRIT BEFORE A FALL.

PROVERBS, OLD TESTAMENT

CHAPTER ONE
THE FIGHTER

Necessity Bonehill grinned and pulled her cap down low on her brow. She raised her fists at the red-faced young man charging towards her like an enraged bull. Stamping her feet on the ground, she widened her stance, enjoying the freedom of the trousers she wore, with so much more room to move than the stupid dresses they forced on her at the Academy.

A weak, dust-filled beam of sunlight sliced through the shadows of the barn. Ness breathed in the mingled scent of summer hay and cattle then, with a gentle exhalation, she sidestepped. The boy staggered past her. He was handsome in a rustic, curly blond hair and suntanned forearms way.

Pity he's such a moron.

She slammed her fist into his ear, making him howl and stumble, crashing into a broken cartwheel that leaned against the barn wall. The small crowd of village lads that had formed a ring around them murmured and shuffled their feet.

'C'mon, Tom,' a thin, pox-faced boy hissed. 'Flatten 'im.'

'Damn tinker,' Tom panted, picking himself up. 'Just you wait till I get 'old of you.'

He charged again. Ness kicked forward, somersaulting over his head and landing behind him just in time to jab her elbow below his kidneys. The watching lads gave an involuntary cheer as their champion fell again, then glanced at each other, shamefaced.

'Get up, Tom. 'E's makin' a fool of yer!' yelled another lad.

With a growl of frustration, Tom stood and swung a huge fist at Ness. He was probably only a year or two older than Ness, fifteen or sixteen, but already a childhood spent working the land had calloused the boy's hands, thickened his sinews. One blow would send Ness sprawling on to the muddy barn floor.

But that wouldn't happen.

Ness snapped her forearms upward, blocking and trapping the oncoming fist. With a pull and a twist, she brought Tom's arm up behind him, bending him double and holding him in a painful armlock. One firm kick from Ness sent him barging out of the ring and straight into the barn door. The satisfying crack echoed around the barn as Tom's skull hit the solid wood. With a grunt, Tom's body went slack and he slumped, unconscious, to the ground.

Ness turned on her heel and faced the gaggle of boys. 'Right,' she panted, fists ready. 'Who's next?'

'Necessity Bonehill! Goodness me! What on *earth* are you doing?' A voice cut through the dusty air and Ness's exhilaration drained away in an instant.

Miss Pinchett.

The head mistress of the Academy stood framed within the side door of the barn. A black silhouette. Shooting Ness a look of disbelief, the boys scurried away, doffing their caps and melting into the shadows of the huge building to search for loose planks in the wall – any means to escape the fierce harpy who strode over to Tom. She looked down her long nose at him, her tight mouth shrinking to a dot.

The boy moaned and sat up as Miss Pinchett jabbed him with the point of her black, polished boot. Looking up, he gave a startled yelp, then jumped to his feet, wincing at the pain.

'You should know better, Tom Roscoe, than to pick on a poor defenceless young lady,' Miss Pinchett said.

'Young lady?' Tom stammered as, grinning, Ness pulled off her cap, spilling thick, black hair over her shoulders. Tom gaped. 'Defenceless?' he whimpered, trying to nurse his bleeding ear and wrenched shoulder at the same time.

'And you can wipe that smug expression from your face this instant, miss,' Pinchett snapped. Her voice stung Ness like whiplash. 'Go immediately to Rookery Heights and wait in my office.'

Gritting her teeth, Ness turned on her heel, stamped out of the barn and across the farm. Her mood darkened as she marched through the woods, kicking out at stones on the rough path.

Ness heaved a sigh as she approached Rookery Heights Academy for Young Ladies. The square building squatted on a rocky outcrop surrounded by marshlands. Its cold square windows stared out to the line of the sea. A low wall edged the scrubby garden. Above her the heavy sky merged into the flat horizon that in turn melted into the washed-out tones of the marsh. Crows cluttered the roof tiles, cawing and bickering.

A horrible place, Ness thought. *What could be worse than lessons in manners and deportment? All that chatter about who is marrying whom and which bachelor is most eligible! That's all the Academy girls think of – marriage*. Ness shivered at the cold. Girls of the Academy were taught to be doe-eyed and cow-brained. Bovine. Ready for the slaughter when they came of age. Ready for marriage to some halfwit lord or baron. Ness spat into the scrubby grass. *Not me*, she thought, stamping her way towards the building.

I can be anyone I want, Ness thought.

An image of Ness's father invaded her thoughts – towering over her in his study, his bloodstone ring glinting red on his finger. '*Only cowards run away from adversity*,' he said.

Pausing at the front door, Ness sighed. *Father would never speak to me again if I ran away. Maybe if I endure one more year here, he'll let me leave.*

*

Miss Pinchett sat in a high-backed chair, her bony fingers interlaced and white at the knuckles. Ness returned her icy stare, arms folded. Bookcases lined the walls, darkening the room. A meagre fire crackled and spat in the hearth. Behind Miss Pinchett stood a small, furtive-looking man. His eyes bulged like a strangled mouse and his face was red and blotchy.

'What are we going to do with you, Necessity Bonehill?' Miss Pinchett sighed, leaning forward over the desk.

'Not a lot, I should imagine,' muttered Ness, picking at her fingernails. 'You could expel me, I suppose.'

'You'd like that, wouldn't you?' Miss Pinchett hissed. Expulsion from Rookery Heights was highly unlikely. Ness knew that. Her father paid a stupid amount of money to keep her here. The Academy couldn't afford to let her go.

'Now that you come to mention it, yes, I would,' Ness said, giving a tight insincere smile. 'But we both know that's not going to happen.'

'No,' Miss Pinchett said, levelling a stony glare at Ness. 'But be warned, Necessity. There will come a point where no amount of money will keep me from excluding you. I can understand why your father wants rid of such an unnatural girl but we shouldn't have to endure such behaviour here at the Academy.'

Ness ground her teeth, tears stinging her eyes. Miss Pinchett dared not take the rod to Ness – but she didn't need to. Her barbed tongue was sharper than any cane and she knew just how to hurt Ness. The clue was in her name. Necessity. Her parents had only had her because they needed to. That's what everybody said. No child, no inheritance. The other night Mollie Rogers had even suggested they had adopted her. She'd paid her back for that.

'Anyway,' Miss Pinchett continued, startling Ness out of her thoughts, 'I'll deal with your flagrant disregard for the rules of this establishment, and of decency itself, another time.' She raised a hand towards the nervous-looking man who stood behind her. 'This is Mr Hardgrave. He's a solicitor. I can hardly see why but he wishes to speak with you.'

Mr Hardgrave scuttled out from behind Miss Pinchett's chair. Under one arm he clutched a small sack. He smoothed back his greasy hair and gave a short bow.

'I have been instructed by my client, Mr Grossford,' he began, glancing around again as if someone might be eavesdropping.

'Uncle Carlos?' Ness gave a smile. *Now there's someone who cares*, she thought. Uncle Carlos sent all kinds of things to her – cake, sweets, books. She hadn't seen him for many years but he used to come to the house when she was a little girl and lived at home. 'Has he sent me a gift?'

'Yes, quite, miss,' coughed Hardgrave, stuffing the sack into Ness's arms. 'I am to hand this sack and the bottle therein –'

'Bottle?' Miss Pinchett frowned. 'I trust there's nothing intoxicating in it?'

'To the best of my knowledge, no,' Hardgrave said, mopping his brow and edging towards the door. 'I shouldn't think so, ma'am.' He turned to Ness. 'I'm to hand it to you personally and instruct you to *never* open it.'

'Never open it? But why?' Ness murmured. She frowned at the sack. The bottle felt hard and cold through the material.

'Haven't the first idea, miss. Now, if you'll excuse me, I must return to London. Good day to you both . . . and good luck!' Hardgrave gave a slight bow and scurried away, slamming the door behind him.

Ness stared down at the sack again.

Miss Pinchett peered at it too. 'Aren't you going to look at it?'

Ness narrowed her eyes at the headmistress. 'Not just yet,' she sniffed. *Not in front of you, you miserable old trout.* With a short smile, Ness hugged the sack to her chest and swept out of the room.

A SOUND HEART IS THE LIFE OF THE FLESH BUT ENVY THE ROTTENNESS OF THE BONES.

PROVERBS, OLD TESTAMENT

CHAPTER TWO
SERGEANT MAJOR MORRIS

With a curse, Ness stormed down the dusty corridors of Rookery Heights and stamped up the stairs, pausing only to kick the head of the moth-eaten tiger-skin rug that covered the entrance-hall floor. Toop, the butler, frowned at her with his hooded eyes. Winifred and Ann, the chambermaids, put their work-reddened hands to their mouths. Winifred gave a feeble curtsy, a coil of red hair springing from her mob cap. Ann's mouth was covered but Ness could see excitement in her blue eyes. They'd be gossiping about Necessity Bonehill in the kitchens tonight, that was for sure.

Ness ignored them. *It's not fair. That old trout Pinchett shouldn't have mentioned my parents*. She slammed herself into the dormitory door, sending it crashing open.

Three girls sat frozen on their beds. Ness glowered at them. Mollie Rogers stared back. She was the nearest in age to Ness, her unruly red hair a testament to her wild temper, but even she knew not to cross Ness when she burst into the room like this. On the bed opposite sat Sarah Devine, eleven, blonde-haired, blue-eyed, and the darling of the Academy.

'Who'd marry *you*, Necessity Bonehill?' Sarah had said on her second day here. 'Your hair is so coarse and black, like a sweep's brush, and your skin is so . . . sunburned.'

The staff had only just managed to persuade Ness not to drop her as she dangled Sarah out of the window by her legs.

Now the youngest, Hannah Downey, fumbled as she slid something under her pillow, desperate not to catch Ness's eye.

Ness strode over to her bed, dropping her own package and pulling Hannah's pillow back.

'What's this then, eh?' Ness said, snatching up a parcel and a letter. 'Papa's been writing again, has he?'

'P-please don't t-take it, Ness.' Hannah's bottom lip began to tremble as she twisted her fingers in her skirts.

'Come on, Ness, she's only nine,' Mollie murmured, kneeling up on her bed.

'Pathetic,' Ness hissed, flashing a warning glance at Mollie. She ripped at the package. A sweet aroma tickled her nose. 'Cake.' Ness smiled and threw it on to her bed next to the sack. She pulled the letter out of the envelope and clambered on to her bed to read it. Hannah's sobs filled the room. 'Stop that snivelling, girl,' Ness snapped. She scanned the paper, icy envy filling her stomach and tightening her throat as she read.

My dearest poppet,

Your last letter so distressed us. Had we known how unhappy you were at Rookery Heights, we would never have made you return after Christmas. Rest assured that we have made arrangements with Miss Pinchett and next weekend Papa and I will come to collect you personally. In the meantime, Cook has made you a cake to share with your friends at the Academy. We have employed a governess so that we can all be together. We're so looking forward to having you back at Squire's Hall.

Your loving mama

Ness stared at the letter. Tears stung her eyes. She felt as if she were falling. Hannah's parents were taking her away from the Academy – *they* cared about their daughter. It wasn't fair!

'Are you all right, Ness?' Hannah said, her faint squeak bringing Ness back.

'Course I am.' Ness stifled a cough and scrubbed an angry fist across her eyes. 'Why wouldn't I be?'

'You're jealous,' Mollie whispered, the realisation dawning on her. 'You're stuck here and Hannah's going home. That's it, isn't it, Ness?'

For a moment Ness stood, uncertain what to do. Hannah gave a stifled sob and leapt from her bed, snatching her letter and cake back.

'Why would I want to be like any of you? You're all

pathetic!' With a snort of contempt, Ness turned and flew from the dormitory.

The light was fading as Ness ran along the path that led from Rookery Heights into the woods. A cool breeze blew in from the sea, making her shiver. *Stupid girls. What does Mollie Rogers know anyway?* Ness snuffled back the sobs that threatened to burst forth. *But they're right, of course,* she thought, picking up a stick and slashing at the undergrowth around her. *What I wouldn't give for a letter like that! All the Christmases, all the summers I've spent rotting in this marshland dump.* True, her parents came to see her every now and then, but since the age of eight, Rookery Heights had been her home.

She wandered on, scything at the grass and bushes. Birds flapped into the trees, chattering at the intrusion. *If only I'd remembered the package,* she thought. *I could have looked at it now.*

A dim light shone through the trees. Ness smiled. As she drew nearer, the familiar outline of the cottage became apparent. Smoke curled from the chimney and an oil lamp burned in the window.

Ness took a step forward.

Then froze.

The cold metal of a gun muzzle chilled the back of her neck, making her draw a sharp breath.

'Who goes there?' said a quavering voice. 'Friend or foe?'

Ness glanced sideways at the strange figure in flannel

pyjamas, with a bristling moustache and grey hair sprouting from under a battered, bullet-holed pith helmet. Sergeant Major Morris.

Ness didn't move. 'It's me, Ness,' she whispered.

'Nick?' the sergeant major said, lowering the gun. 'Is it you?' Dropping the weapon, he threw his arms around Ness. 'Thank goodness, boy! I haven't seen you for years!'

'It's Ness, and I saw you yesterday,' she said, grinning.

'Did you?' The sergeant major scratched his head, pushing back the helmet to reveal his thinning hair and ruddy complexion. 'What was I doing?'

'Teaching me to fight,' Ness said, half crouching and jabbing a playful fist at the old man. 'As usual.'

Over the years he'd taught her boxing, sword craft, rifle shooting, all spiced with tales of his regiment, the Hinderton Rifles, and his time in India. He looked old but he wasn't frail and he was fast. He was the one person who made life at the Academy bearable.

'I was, eh? Good show, good show!' Morris barked and gave Ness a sly wink. 'Come inside and have some tea. Getting dark. You don't know what might be lurking about.'

Ness watched Morris march off into the clearing and up the overgrown path to the front of the cottage.

'He's mad,' Mollie had said one night. 'You can hear him sometimes, screaming in the dark, firing his rifle at shadows.'

'He lost his family in the Indian Mutiny,' Sarah

whispered. 'Watched his daughter and grandchildren die, trapped in a burning house.'

'Miss Pinchett has declared the cottage out of bounds to all girls,' Mollie had said, with a shudder.

Which was why Ness had sought it out in the first place.

'Well?' Morris said, as he stopped and pushed the door open. 'Are you coming in?'

Inside, the cottage looked strangely ordered but still as dusty and faded as its owner. Books lined the shelves, squeezed together tightly. Ness had tried to pull down a book on swordsmanship once and nearly been buried in an avalanche of other titles. A small table huddled by the fire, surrounded by four wooden stools. Clothes hung on the backs of doors and flags draped from the walls. At the side of the door, four rifles stood sentry next to each other.

Above the fireplace, a ragged standard hung from the chimney breast, with guns crossed over a leering demon's face and fiery gold letters that declared, *Fourth Hinderton Rifles: Satan, Do Your Worst*. Ness often puzzled over this flag but all Morris would ever say was, 'Hindertons, my old regiment. Unique, we were.' And he would stiffen to attention for a second.

'So, Nick, what brings you here on such a dark night?' Morris said, planting himself on a stool and leaning forward to stare at Ness.

'I can't bear it at the Academy any longer,' Ness sighed, leaning on the table. 'Why did my parents send me here? Do they really care about me so little?'

Morris's eyes twinkled in the firelight. 'Sometimes parents have to make hard choices,' he whispered hoarsely.

'Hard choices? Such as keeping me in a dump like this?' Ness muttered.

'Sit tight,' Morris said. 'You're safe here. They won't get you here.' But he leaned closer towards her, a haunted look in his eye. 'They lurk in every shadow of the empire.'

'What d'you mean?' Ness said, her voice faint.

Morris stared at her blankly for a second, then shook himself and glanced out of the window. 'Toop's out there looking for you,' he murmured.

Ness peered out into the darkness. A faint glimmer of a storm lantern flickered between the branches.

'How d'you know it's Toop?' Ness said, blinking to see the faint light.

'The man has a limp,' Morris said, winking. 'The lamp swings awkwardly. Besides, *Miss Pinchett* wouldn't come out in the dark looking for you.'

'I'd better go,' Ness said.

'Keep your wits about you,' Morris said, opening the door.

'I can get past Toop.' Ness grinned.

'It's not Toop I'm worried about,' Morris called after her as she plunged into the darkness.

With wishing comes grieving.

Traditional proverb

CHAPTER THREE

AN UNWELCOME VISITOR

A sliver of bright moonlight illuminated the slumbering shapes in the dormitory as Ness crept back in. She could make out Hannah's face, serene, secure in the knowledge that she was loved and would soon be going home. The heaviness in Ness's heart returned. Her trembling hands rattled the iron bedhead as she grabbed it to steady herself after her headlong flight through the woods. Her heart pounded. As she had predicted, Toop had been easy to evade, but Morris's parting words had unsettled her.

The bottle still lay on Ness's bed, and she slid it out from the rough sack. It felt solid and icy cold. She couldn't tell whether it was made of thick glass or metal but even in the half-light, Ness could make out the dancing figures that decorated the main body of the bottle – hideous heads with horns and leering faces. She shuddered.

Are they a warning? She traced a finger along the neck of the bottle, which ended in a snarling dragon's head, jaws wide, the stopper clamped between its teeth.

'I can't decide if you're horrible or beautiful,' she whispered.

Why would Uncle Carlos send her something like this and tell her never to open it? Ness shook the bottle. No liquid swirled within; nothing rattled. As far as she could tell, it was empty. She sighed, placing it on her pillow, then undressed, wriggling into her thick nightdress. *It must be one of Uncle Carlos's jokes.* Ness always remembered him laughing, usually in the hallway at home when she was young. Her parents never laughed though. She'd never thought of that before. She could remember Uncle Carlos smiling up at her as she peered through the banister rails, with Father scowling at him.

'Your father doesn't appreciate my sense of humour, my little Necessity,' he had called up once. 'He knows that I will always have the last laugh.'

Ness had grinned back, not knowing what he meant. He was just teasing Father, she supposed.

She held the bottle up in front of her. She gave the stopper half a twist and flinched. With a nervous laugh, she dropped the bottle in her lap. *This is ridiculous. What did I expect would happen?*

The dormitory door clicked open and Miss Pinchett peered into the shadows of the room on her nightly patrol. Stuffing the bottle under her pillow, Ness rolled over, eyes squeezed shut. *I'll open it tomorrow*, she thought, as the door closed and drowsiness overcame her.

The events of the day swirled around her mind and spilled into dreams. Ness was a small child again, dancing, twirling, holding tightly on to her mother's neck. She could see her mother's blonde hair, smell her perfume as they waltzed across the room.

'One day you'll meet a handsome prince.' Mother smiled. Her blue eyes sparkled with love and affection.

'Like how you met Father?' Ness asked, but she couldn't hear her mother's answer.

The dream shifted. Mother sat tearfully at the end of her bed.

'You have to go, Necessity,' Mother said, her voice hoarse. 'Your father's right. It's for your own good.'

'But why?' Necessity asked.

'One day, you may understand,' Mother said, rising from the bed. 'You will learn, but for now you must do as we tell you and leave us.'

'But I don't want to go,' Ness sobbed, throwing herself at her mother. 'I want to stay here with you . . .'

A creaking floorboard scraped across her dream, dragging Ness to wakefulness. Someone was moving about among the beds. The shadows were thick but Ness could hear the stealthy tread. Close. Moonlight flashed on a cruelly curved blade, making Ness catch her breath. The silhouette of a hooded figure slipped across the square of the window.

Wisdom often exists under a shabby coat.

Traditional proverb

CHAPTER FOUR

INJUSTICE

Ness lay still, but her heart pounded so hard she thought the intruder would hear it. She held her breath as a shadow loomed over her. Her eyes were more accustomed to the dark now and she saw a face wrapped in a scarf. Only the dark eyes could be seen.

Ness lunged forward but the bedclothes dragged at her, restricting her movement. With a muffled hiss, the stranger pulled back, turned and scurried towards the open sash window. Giving a brief, backward glance, the intruder leapt out into the night.

Ness wrestled with the heavy sheets and blankets that seemed intent on pinning her in the bed. She rushed over just in time to see the dark figure sprinting across the front lawn towards the marshes.

'You don't get away that easily,' she muttered under her breath, pulling on a pair of Sarah's slippers and swinging her legs out of the window. She clambered out into the cold night air, glancing back into the room. The girls had slept through the intrusion. *Good*, Ness thought. At least they won't alert old Pinchett.

The drop seemed perilously high to Ness. She marvelled at how the intruder had managed to throw himself out without breaking an ankle. Her progress wasn't half as fluid or acrobatic. A rusty drainpipe ran down the wall just beside the window and Ness clung to this, inching her way towards the ground. Finally, she was rewarded with the sting of gravel beneath her feet and she launched herself off after the stranger.

Ness rushed across the lawn and down the marsh road. Her nightdress tangled in her legs, forcing her to gather it up. The silver birches that lined the road looked blue in the bright moonlight. She glimpsed a movement up ahead. The intruder had slowed his pace thinking he wouldn't be followed. Ness gave a hiss of triumph, but the dark figure turned at the sound and sprinted up the road.

Ness hurried after him. The figure began to widen the distance between them, then suddenly swerved into the woods that lined one side of the road. At the same time, Ness's nightdress tangled itself around her left leg again, sending her spiralling to the ground. Struggling to her feet, she swept the dirt from her nightclothes and plunged into the shadows of the woods.

Darkness pressed in on Ness. Here and there, shafts of moonlight formed pillars between the tree trunks, illuminating small clearings but deepening the gloom around them. Brambles snagged at her nightdress. Ness stopped and shivered. She suddenly became aware of the cold, the thin soles of her slippers. The stranger couldn't be far away – hiding in the dark, knife at the ready. A twig snapped behind her.

'I know you're out there,' Ness said. Her voice sounded brittle and dry. She tried to keep it calm. 'Why don't you come out and fight?'

Silence. Ness stood holding her breath, but nothing moved.

Suddenly feeling vulnerable, she glanced around. The woods looked different at night but she knew she wasn't far from Morris's cottage. Hugging herself, she waded through the undergrowth towards her safe haven.

Sergeant Major Morris was standing on the roof of his cottage when Ness arrived. He was holding a telescope to one eye and staring out across the tops of the trees.

'Major Morris?' Ness called up. 'It's me. What are you looking at?'

Morris didn't seem to hear her at first but then lowered the telescope and blinked down at her. 'Ah, Nick, back again? I'm not sure what it is just yet,' he said, sounding troubled. 'A sail . . .'

'A sail?' Ness frowned.

'Mmm,' Morris muttered, beckoning her to join him.

Ness clambered up the ladder that leaned against the side of the cottage and Morris handed her the telescope. She squinted through it at the distant moonlit horizon.

Little stood out against the blue and silver shadows of the marshes – only a few birds flying past.

Ness shrugged but Morris gently nudged the telescope a little to her right. She could just make out a tall prow and a triangular sail poking above the black silhouettes of the reed beds that lined the marsh.

'I've not seen that kind of sail before,' Morris said. 'Not round these parts.'

'It doesn't look like a barge,' Ness said. 'Too small.'

'Looks foreign to me,' Morris murmured. 'Could be trouble.' He climbed down and strode into the cottage.

'Trouble?' Ness said, following him. 'I wonder if it has anything to do with the intruder in our room.'

Morris stopped dead. 'Intruder?' he said without turning round.

'Yes,' Ness said warily, remembering his strange outburst earlier that night. 'Someone was sneaking around our dormitory. He had a strange scarf covering his face and a curved knife. He looked foreign to me.'

'What happened?' Morris turned, his face pale.

'I saw him off.' Ness couldn't help grinning. 'I chased him into the woods – that's how I came to be here.'

'Good lad,' Morris said, patting Ness on the shoulder, but he didn't smile back. 'What would he be after, I wonder?'

Ness shrugged. 'Can't think,' she said. 'I haven't anything worth stealing. It's all very odd. First that solicitor yesterday, then –'

'Solicitor?' Morris said, his face twitching.

'Yes, from Uncle Carlos,' Ness said. 'He sent me some old bottle. It looks horrible –'

'Carlos? A bottle?' Morris barked, grabbing Ness by the wrist with an iron grip.

'Yes. Ow! Major Morris, you're hurting me!'

Morris yanked her so close she could see the silver stubble on his chin, a fleck of spit on his lip. 'Where's the bottle now? Where?'

'At the dormitory,' Ness cried, becoming afraid as she noticed his wide eyes and trembling hand. 'Why? What's so special about an empty bottle?'

Before Morris could reply, the door crashed open.

'There he is, constable. Arrest that man!' Miss Pinchett cried, stepping into the cottage.

Two burly men in blue tunics and white trousers barged past her and grabbed Morris by the arms. Morris turned and backhanded one of them, sending him stumbling into Miss Pinchett.

'Stay calm now, Sergeant. We just want to ask a few questions,' the other constable said, struggling to hold on to Morris.

'He broke into the Academy tonight, officer,' Miss Pinchett gasped, scrambling to her feet. 'I don't know what's missing yet but I saw him running across the lawn and this young lady was following – acting as an accomplice, no doubt!'

'Ridiculous!' Morris spat and turned to face the constable.

'Look, old-timer,' the constable grumbled. 'I'm not

'appy about bein' dragged from me bed at this unearthly hour, but it looks suspicious to me, so if you'll just come quietly –'

'It wasn't him!' Ness cried.

'Don't listen to her – she's completely hysterical,' Miss Pinchett screeched. 'She was wearing trousers yesterday!'

For a moment the constable stared at Ness, trying to take in what Miss Pinchett had just said.

'Now, look here, I haven't been near Rookery Heights,' Morris insisted, but the other man had picked himself up and rapped the sergeant major sharply on the back of the head with his truncheon. Ness gave a scream as Morris slumped to the floor and threw herself down next to him.

'Major Morris! Are you all right?' she sobbed, massaging his shoulder.

'Go to your parents, Ness. Take the bottle,' Morris groaned. 'Don't let it out of your sight.'

One of the constables dragged Ness back as the other pinned Morris's arms and locked irons around his wrists.

'What are you going to do with him?' Ness asked.

'We'll ask him a few questions,' the constable said, giving a gap-toothed grin. 'Miss Pinchett seems sure he's our intruder.'

'But she wasn't there,' Ness snapped, struggling against the other constable's grip. 'How could she know?'

'Now that's enough, missy,' the constable barked, pulling Morris to his feet.

The sergeant major swayed a little as he stood. Elbowing

herself free, Ness threw herself at the constable who held Morris.

'Ness!' Morris hissed, stopping her dead.

'You know my real name?' Ness said, frowning.

Morris leaned forward, his face close to hers. Ness could feel his breath on her ear.

'No time to explain now,' he whispered. 'Get the bottle, go to the quay and ask for a Jacob Carr. He has a barge that will take you to London. Find your parents, Ness.'

'That'll do,' the constable said, pulling cruelly on Morris's wrist irons. 'You're coming with us.'

Ness stood helpless as the constables manhandled Morris out of the cottage. She listened as their footsteps faded into the depths of the woods.

Miss Pinchett blocked the doorway, arms folded, a self-satisfied grin on her face. 'Now, Necessity Bonehill,' she hissed, 'it's back to Rookery Heights for you. Or do I have to call the constables back to carry you there?'

Ness ignored Miss Pinchett and stared out of the cottage into the shadows of the woods. Someone had peered at her from the undergrowth and then vanished. But Ness had glimpsed dark, fierce eyes and a face obscured by a black headscarf.

If wishes were true, shepherds would be kings.

Traditional proverb

CHAPTER FIVE

THE BOTTLE

All the way back to the Academy, Ness sensed that they were being followed, but the figure in the undergrowth didn't reappear. *Major Morris said to go back to the Academy*, Ness thought. *He said my real name! Things are getting stranger by the hour.*

Miss Pinchett walked in stony silence. Ness's heart felt like lead when she thought of Morris being taken away. *What will they do with him? It's not fair*. Ness glowered at the headmistress.

Rookery Heights looked more forlorn than ever as they crunched up the gravel pathway to its front door. More black birds huddled on the roof top, cawing and mocking Ness. Toop stood at the doorway in his dressing gown and stared at her with disdain.

'Go back upstairs to bed, Necessity,' Miss Pinchett said, taking an oil lamp from Toop. 'And don't wake the girls. We'll see what's missing in the morning and discuss your role in the burglary then.'

Ness opened her mouth to protest, but Miss Pinchett swept away across the hall. She took the lamp with her, leaving only moonlight to see by.

Ness stamped upstairs. She didn't care who she woke.

Back in the dormitory, Ness threw herself on to her bed, pulling the covers over her. The bottle clinked against the bed under her pillow. Ness pulled it out. Maybe this was what the intruder was after. Morris had told her not to let it out of her sight. Maybe it was valuable after all.

Ness shook it next to her ear. Nothing.

If it was empty, why couldn't she open it? It looked old – maybe it would disintegrate. Ness had read of antiquarians who opened ancient tombs only to watch the contents crumble to dust when they came into contact with the open air. Maybe the bottle was held together by the stopper. She flicked the side of the bottle and listened to the clink. *It sounds strong enough. If there is something inside, maybe it'll give me a clue about what's going on!*

But the bottle looked horrible; the leering, dancing figures around its body seemed to mock her. It felt horrible too – cold and heavy. Her stomach still fluttered and she shivered despite the blankets. *What would Father say?*

'He'd tell me to stop fooling about,' she muttered, scowling. 'Don't send someone a bottle if you don't want it opened!'

She snatched it up and gave the lid a final tug.

The stopper opened with a hollow *pop*.

Only the girls' gentle breathing broke the silence.

Ness gasped. A dim light began to glow from inside the bottle accompanied by a distant scream that became louder and louder. Ness dropped the bottle and covered her ears.

Smoke boiled from the bottle's mouth, tainting the room with a foul smell of decay. For a moment, a hideous figure filled Ness's vision. Gaunt and skeletal, stretching and twisting its body in agony, the figure spiralled out of the bottle's neck. With long, scaly arms clamped around its head, it screamed. Brown, serrated teeth lined the ragged mouth, and its eyes were screwed tightly shut like some hideous newborn baby.

And then, in an explosion of light, it vanished. The scream turned into a deafening roar that filled Ness's ears as she was hurled against the dormitory wall. Windows shattered, glass showering over her. Beds bounced across the room, spilling their sleeping occupants. Mattresses and pillows split, sending a blizzard of feathers into the air. Then, suddenly, the noise stopped. Ness slid down the wall and fell to the floor as darkness took her.

A freezing coldness enveloped Ness. Her head throbbed and bulged as if it would explode. Smoke billowed and swirled around the room, mixing with the storm of duck down. Ness could just see the slumped outlines of Mollie and Sarah on the floor. But something else floated between her and the other girls. Somewhere in the near distance, the creature shifted and flickered in and out of her vision. It looked like a hideous puppet or a doll.

'I am the djinn of one thousand contagions,' he said, his voice reedy and mocking. 'You have freed me. I am grateful. What would you wish for, child?'

Ness felt the weight of her own body as she tried to shift herself up off the floor. 'What would I wish for?' she croaked. Her tongue filled her mouth, raw and painful.

'I will grant you one wish.' The djinn gave a needle-toothed grin, cocking his tiny head to one side.

This is a dream, Ness thought. *A bad dream.* Sweat slicked her palm despite the cold she felt. Her whole body shivered. *What would I wish for?*

'I wish,' Ness gasped, the words wheezing through her constricted throat, 'I wish my parents loved me.'

'Are you sure they don't already, Necessity?' The djinn's face swam closer and Ness could see the crusted scabs around the stitches that closed his eyes; the waxy, leprous skin that peeled from his forehead. 'Is that what you really want? You could have wealth, power, Miss Pinchett's head on a stick . . .'

Bile rose in Ness's throat. She felt so weary. 'My parents don't love me,' she whispered. 'They left me here to rot. I wish they loved me and then I could go home.'

'A waste of a wish, Necessity Bonehill,' the djinn said, leering at her. 'If that is what you want, so be it. But be warned – people love for different reasons.'

'What do you mean?' Ness said, shaking her head.

'You'll see,' the djinn said, giving an unpleasant laugh. 'In seven days' time your wish will be granted, but it will cost you everything . . .'

The smoke spiralled and boiled around the djinn as he grew smaller and more distant. His cackling faded into the night and Ness was left leaning against the cracked plaster of her dormitory wall.

A chill breeze blew in through the empty window frames, making the ragged curtains billow. Ness shook herself. The pain, the roughness of her throat, her throbbing head all subsided as if she had never felt them.

'It must have been a dream,' she whispered to herself.

But the wrecked room was real enough. Not a stick of furniture lay intact nor in its proper place. Beds were upended, chests of drawers were on their sides, spilling contents across the scorched floor. Ness stifled a sob of horror.

There, tangled in their bedding, lay Hannah, Mollie and Sarah. Sweat matted their hair, plastering it to their heads as they shivered feverishly. They stared into the shadows, delirious, panting for breath through blue lips.

Wincing, Ness crept over to Mollie, and gently shook her shoulder. It was no good. She stared blankly, with no hint of recognition. Ness knelt among her stricken schoolmates and wept, her whole body shuddering. This was her fault. There must have been something in the bottle. And she had let it out.

Miss Pinchett appeared at the splintered door, her face pale, her mouth wide in disbelief.

'Oh my Lord,' she whispered, hurrying forward and scooping up Hannah's frail form. 'What happened? Hannah? Can you hear me?' She hugged the little girl to her. Hannah's head lolled to one side, her breath rattling from cracked lips.

'I don't know.' Ness's voice quivered as she spoke. 'I opened the bottle and . . .'

But Miss Pinchett wasn't listening. She glared at Ness. 'You did this, Necessity Bonehill,' she hissed through gritted teeth. 'You've poisoned these poor children and I'll see you hang for it!'

Ingratitude is the daughter of pride.

Traditional proverb

CHAPTER SIX
JACOB CARR

Miss Pinchett's face twisted with hatred as she spat her accusations at her.

'You horrible malicious girl,' she snarled. 'You've been trouble ever since you came to this place.'

'No, it wasn't my fault. I –' Ness began, stepping back and nearly tripping over a splintered chair leg.

'You made these girls' lives a misery,' Miss Pinchett continued, her voice low. 'You've done as you pleased, gone where you liked and now you've sunk to this. But mark my words, you will pay dear!'

'Please, Miss Pinchett,' Ness sobbed, desperate not to look at the poor girls groaning and shivering on the floor. 'I meant no harm.'

'Toop!' Miss Pinchett yelled, laying Hannah down and hurrying to the door. 'Winifred! Send for the constables! Fetch the doctor!'

Ness's heart pounded in her chest. For the first time

in her life she felt truly frightened – even the encounter with the intruder had been edged with excitement. If Miss Pinchett was sending for the constables they'd take her away and hang her! She glanced around the shattered room. *I can't stay here. Who was it Major Morris said to find? Jacob Carr at the quay?*

Snatching the open bottle and the stopper from the floor, Ness barged past Miss Pinchett and down the stairs. The house was in turmoil. Girls screamed. Somewhere Toop was shouting something to the chambermaids. In a blur of panic, Ness found herself at the front door.

The cold night air prickled the back of Ness's neck as the rough driveway stung her bare feet. A few crows disturbed by the chaos flapped and complained above her. Once more Ness ran, only this time she was leaving the Academy for good.

The cries behind her grew more distant but her own breathing sounded loud and urgent as she pounded down the lane towards the village and the quay. She was sure she could hear footsteps behind her. Had the creature come back to get her? Or was it the intruder with his cruel knife? Every shadow along the muddy lane seemed to move and swirl. Ness stumbled and tripped, crying out as branches reached for her from the hedgerows, snagging her nightdress and hair. She glanced back at Rookery Heights to see that lamps had been lit. Toop or one of the maids would be hurrying behind her to get help from the village. Ness ran on. The lane ran into a path that snaked down to the quay. Ness could see the bulk of a barge, black against the moonlit water.

A figure loomed out of the darkness, spreading its arms and making Ness scream. She lashed out but found herself enveloped in a tight bear hug.

'Whoa, steady, miss! You'll lay someone low with those fists of yours,' the figure said, his voice soft. 'Now what's all the hurry and why's a young lady like you skipping around in the dark in nothin' more than a nightie?'

'Who are you?' Ness panted. Nausea pressed at her throat again.

She looked up at a square block of a man. His flat nose and stocky build made him look like a fierce giant but gentle blue eyes smiled out beneath his stern brow.

'Jacob Carr's me name,' said the bargeman, relaxing his grip and extending a palm as Ness dropped back into a standing position. 'Skipper of the *Galopede*, fastest barge on the Thames.' He smiled.

Ness stifled a sob. 'Jacob Carr?' she said, her voice weak. Her head throbbed and her muscles ached from the sprint down the lane. 'Thank goodness! My name is Necessity Bonehill. I need to go to my parents . . . in London . . . Major Morris said you'd take me.'

'Charlie Morris?' Carr said, his face growing solemn. 'Is there trouble then?'

'Yes,' Ness gasped. The world swam before her. She swayed and grabbed Carr's shoulder.

'You need to sit down,' the bargeman said.

Ness allowed herself to be guided along the rough, overgrown quayside. To her right the marshes lay swathed in darkness and she could only see the shadowy bulk of the barge, sails furled, rigging rattling gently in the night breeze. Carr led her across the gangplank, on to the deck and down into the cabin. He sat her down on the rough pallet bed and squatted in front of her.

'You're lucky you came when you did,' he said. His face was weather-beaten, careworn, and flecks of silver streaked his dark, curly hair, but Ness couldn't have put an age on him. 'I was about to set sail. If Morris told you to come 'ere, then that's good enough for me. You rest – you seem exhausted. We'll 'ave you back in London in no time.'

Ness laid her head on the pillow while Jacob disappeared up top. She could hear him calling orders to someone, feet thumping on the deck above. The barge began to creak and Ness knew they were moving away from Rookery Heights and its horrors. A tear squeezed itself out of the corner of her eye. She gritted her teeth and tried not to think of the other girls, shivering and fever-ridden. It was too horrible. Her throat tightened as the realisation dawned on her once more. *It's all my fault – I opened that bottle . . .*

'Don't cry,' Ness told herself, hugging the pillow. 'Don't you dare cry.'

Ness awoke to the pitch and roll of the barge. Daylight filtered in through the hatch above her. The smell of tar and the sea filled her nostrils – she could almost taste them. She glanced around the tiny, cluttered cabin. Charts spread across the table lay pinned down by pewter mugs, lanterns and books. Boxes filled one corner, stacked and leaning perilously over the table. It was a wonder everything didn't come crashing down. There among the clutter sat the bottle. Unstoppered. Accusing her.

Her body ached and a deep sadness seemed to weigh her down. On a stool by the bed lay a pile of clothes. She moved slowly, dragging the clothes on. The thick woollen skirts and jumper were a little musty and moth-eaten but they felt warm. A pair of small boots with a hole in the soles stood next to the stool. With one of Carr's thick jackets pulled over her, she clambered up the ladder to the deck.

It was a bright day but the breeze chilled her. The river stretched off into the horizon as the barge skipped across the water, rust-red sails snapping in the wind. Ness listened to the creak of wood and rope and the hiss of the river as the vessel cut through the water. Jacob Carr stood at the helm and a small, angry-looking man scurried about securing ropes and pulling on the tarpaulin that covered the cargo on deck.

'Mornin', Miss Bonehill.' Carr smiled. 'I hope you're feelin' better.'

'Yes, thank you, Mr Carr, considering all that happened last night,' Ness said, shivering.

'You found the clothes I left for you?' Jacob said. 'The last of my daughter Susan's gear. A bit old now but they'll do the job.'

'They're very . . . warm,' she said with a weak smile.

Something in his open manner made Ness want to

share what had happened. She found herself telling Jacob Carr everything, even about the bottle and the djinn in her strange dream. It all came out in a torrent, every detail. Carr listened, his face impassive.

Finally Ness gave a sigh. 'It all sounds so fantastical. You probably think I'm mad.'

Carr shook his head. 'I've plied these 'ere waters for long enough to know there's more to the world than what's in front of you. I only hope Morris is faring well. He knows how to look after himself though. Manny and I 'ave seen some rare old sights in the past, eh, Manny?'

Ness turned with a start. The angry-looking man had been standing closer to her than she'd realised.

He gave a snort. 'Cursed, she is,' he snapped, his steely blue eyes glaring at her from under bushy eyebrows. 'Watch her.' He stalked off, tugging at a few ropes as he passed them.

Ness stared after him. 'Cursed?' she murmured. 'What did he mean by that?'

'Don't mind Manny.' Carr grinned. 'He don't mean no harm. Just a touch melodramatic, that's all. We once rescued a young girl, just like you, from the water and Manny was all for throwin' her back. Reckoned she was a mermaid.' He rolled his eyes. 'Besides, you're wearing a pair of his old boots so he doesn't think you're all bad. We'll have you back safe with your parents in no time.'

Ness nodded. When they heard what had happened perhaps her parents would be so relieved she was unharmed that everything would be all right between them again. And what if the djinn had granted her wish? They would welcome her with open arms, surely!

The morning wore on and Ness watched the distant riverbanks float by. She tried not to wonder what was happening at Rookery Heights or where Morris was, so she concentrated instead on the hissing and splashing around the bow of the barge. At one point Ness glanced behind her and felt a chill. In the distance, to their starboard side, a triangular sail fluttered.

'Mr Carr,' she called up the barge, 'what kind of boat is that?'

Jacob squinted at the sail in the distance. 'Can't rightly say,' he called back. 'Not like anything we usually see on the river. What d'you reckon, Manny?'

'Dunno,' Manny scowled, shading his eyes with his hands. 'Small. Fast. Peculiar.'

The sail grew larger but the craft kept a distance so Ness could only just make out the dark figures of its occupants.

'Well, they look to be passin' us and leavin' us alone,' Carr said gruffly.

Ness watched the sail gradually disappear up the river ahead of them.

The river grew busier as it narrowed. Other barges skipped through the waves, their captains waving to Carr. Larger vessels came into view and the air took on a smoky, tarry taste.

'We're nearly in London,' Carr announced.

Ness stared at the pall of black smog in the distance. She hadn't been home for at least five years. Her heart fluttered. *What will Mama and Father say? How will I explain what's happened? They must know something about it all – about Carlos and the bottle*. She bit her lip.

More boats and barges, ships and skiffs cluttered the river. Solid brick-built quays began to replace the earthen reed beds that had lined the river's edge. Manny scurried about, securing stays on the cargo, calling waspishly to other craft that came too close. Soon they were tying up at a dock that was overshadowed by tall warehouses.

Ness sniffed at the smoky air. *London*, she thought.

Part the Second

London

Death drives a fast carriage.

Traditional proverb

CHAPTER SEVEN
A SHOCKING DISCOVERY

'We'll be here for a few more hours before we head back to the coast in case you need us, miss,' Jacob said, as they stood on the dockside. Gangs of burly men swarmed over the *Galopede*, offloading sacks and crates.

Ness smiled. 'Thank you, Mr Carr, but once I'm home I'll be fine.' He'd been too kind already, even sharing a meagre breakfast of ham and eggs. Jacob hadn't seemed to mind, but Manny's glare had drifted between his old boots and the tiny flake of meat on his platter.

'Well, take care. Are you sure you won't take the price of a cab to get you home?' Carr said, a frown creasing his tanned face.

'Thank you, Mr Carr, but my parents are more than able to pay for it. I wouldn't dream of taking any more from you,' Ness said, laying a hand on Carr's arm. 'And thank you again.'

'Keep that bottle safe,' Carr said. He'd given her a sack to wrap it in to protect it from prying eyes.

'Best be off then.' Manny scowled at her over Jacob's shoulder.

Jacob laughed and patted Ness's hand before turning to bellow at one of the dockers who had dropped a crate.

Ness watched the men scurrying about for a moment; bewhiskered sailors elbowed through a gang of Chinese workers heaving on black-tarred rope as they winched a bale over the side of a barge. Rigging and masts formed a dense jungle that pressed against the blackened brick of the dock-side warehouses. Shouts and laughter grated on her ears. It had been five or more years since she had been in London and the memory of the silent, desolate marshes seemed unreal in this churning mass of humanity. *At least the air at the Academy didn't choke me*, Ness thought as she put the sack on her back and squeezed past a street seller hawking caged birds.

Taverns and nautical outfitters lined the streets leading up from the dock. Old seamen nursed their flagons and chewed on pipes, eyeing passers-by suspiciously, while toothless women in gaudy silken gowns with ribbons drooping in their hair called out to passing sailors.

Searching around for a hansom cab, Ness caught a glimpse of a boy about her age. He was dressed in a rather military style tunic and a turban covered most of his black hair. For a second, their gazes met. Ness instantly recognised his fierce glare. She lunged forward, ready to challenge him, but the boy threw himself into the crowd and vanished from sight.

Ness hurried on as the streets widened and she marched away from the river. 'Not a cab to be found,' she tutted to herself, glancing over her shoulder. Hopefully the boy wouldn't dare attack with so many people around. The odd carriage or coach did clatter past but each was occupied and the drivers ignored her calls.

The clothes of passers-by became cleaner, more genteel. Ness nodded and smiled to a group of ladies who stared straight through her in her scruffy river-girl's clothes.

At last a hansom cab stood by the roadside. Its horse drooped and slumped in the middle. The driver, wrapped in a huge weather-stained coat, slouched in the sprung seat at the back of the carriage, picking his bulbous red nose. Ness gave a cough and the man gazed down from his seat but continued burrowing with his finger.

'Could you take me to Bonehill House on Brompton Road?' she asked.

'Could do,' the driver muttered in a disgusting, nasal voice, pulling his finger out and rolling what he'd found into a ball. 'You got money?'

'No, but my father, Mr Anthony Bonehill, does – lots of it,' Ness snapped, raising her head imperiously and staring straight into the driver's eyes. 'He'll pay you handsomely for bringing me home.'

The driver looked at her properly and jumped down, wiping his fingers on his grubby coat as he landed. 'Forgive me, miss,' he said, pulling open the door to the cab and touching the brim of his hat. 'It's just, well, your dress, like . . . It's not, I mean, I can tell by yer voice that yer genteel, like, but –'

'Never mind that,' Ness said, glancing around once and then clambering in, wrinkling her nose at the musty mildewed smell that mingled with the polished leather upholstery. 'My father will be wondering where I am. Get a move on, please.'

The cab bounced and squeaked as the driver got into the rear seat and flicked his whip at the horse. Ness leaned forward to peer out of the covered passenger compartment just in time to see the boy in the turban breaking cover from the crowd. He skidded to a halt and looked helplessly from right to left as if searching for a ride himself. Ness threw herself back in the cab and banged on the ceiling.

'Faster, man, faster,' she snapped at the driver above. She was being followed, that much was certain. She had to lose him and get home.

The cab rocked along the grimy streets but Ness barely noticed the passing neighbourhoods. Her stomach fluttered. She was excited about seeing home again and yet a cold dread filled her too. Her old bedroom stood out clear in her memory, as did the study where Miss Cheem the governess had taught her. In her mind's eye, she swept into the hallway with its tiled floor and grand staircase. Rowson, the head butler, would stand to attention, arm crooked ready to receive coats. Ness gave a slight smile.

'Here we are, miss, Brompton Road,' the driver called down, snapping her out of her thoughts. He said something else but Ness wasn't listening.

Instead of gazing up at her home, she stared at the pile of smouldering masonry and timber that sprawled where Bonehill House once stood.

The smell of smoke filled the air and a crowd of ragged urchins scrambled over the charred beams and crumbling stonework. They tiptoed in bare feet through hot ash searching for anything worth salvaging.

Ness jumped out of the cab. She staggered over a heap of rubble and ran through what used to be the front door, grabbing at the nearest boy, who cradled a charred satchel in his arms.

'Get away,' she screamed, snatching the satchel and almost hurling him bodily behind her. 'What are you doing?'

'Leave it out,' yelled another boy in rags. 'There's fine pickings to be 'ad 'ere an' no mistake.'

Ness advanced on him. 'Not while I'm here,' she snarled, raising a fist. 'This is my house and you've no right to be here!'

The boy rubbed his cheek and weighed Ness up. He backed off, then gave a whistle and the other children scurried after him.

Beyond them she saw a young girl in a maid's uniform, tugging at a silver tray that poked from beneath a pile of bricks. She recognised the tiles of what would have been the reception hall, but they were cracked and grey, peeping through gaps in a thick coating of ash.

'What happened? Where is everyone?' Ness asked the girl. 'Where are Mr and Mrs Bonehill? Are they . . . Did they get out?'

The maid looked up, dazed, her face streaked with ash. 'I dunno,' she said, wiping her eye with the back of her hand. 'It happened in the night. Master and Mistress were all tucked up, then the next minute it was all smoke an' flames.' The maid shuddered. 'I wouldn't 'ave come back, only my husband, he said there might be somethin' left behind that's worth havin'. I said I wouldn't come back 'ere for all the tea in China after I saw that . . . that . . . thing . . . but he made me.'

'Thing?' Ness repeated, clutching the satchel to her.

'It was 'orrible,' the maid whispered. 'A hideous creature dancin' through the flames, like a little doll made of bones. No one believed me, mind.'

'A little doll?' Ness felt as if she were falling down a deep well. The thing that came out of the bottle, the djinn, had been here . . .

A shadow fell across her and she gazed up at the driver.

'Beggin' yer pardon, miss,' he said, feeding the brim of his hat through his fingers. 'I know this is a delicate time an' all but it was a long journey 'cross town an' I was wonderin', if yer don't need takin' elsewhere, I'll 'ave me money now please.'

'I don't know where anyone is,' Ness murmured. 'I don't even know if they're alive or dead.'

'I do need my fare, with it bein' so far an' all.' The driver edged closer.

Ness's mind cleared and she frowned at the driver. 'You're asking me for payment at a time like this?' Fury boiled up inside her.

'Well, with all due respect, I didn't burn your 'ouse down,' the driver said, his voice hardening. 'Or aren't you who you say yer are?'

'I don't know what you mean,' Ness snapped back.

'Yeah, that would be a clever old ruse, that would.' The driver leered at her. 'Trick me into drivin' you all across town to a place you know 'as just burnt down recent, like.'

'How dare you?' Ness stared at the man. His lopsided grin, his round nose and yellowed teeth revolted her.

'Oh, I wasn't born yesterday, missy,' he sneered. 'Excuse me, miss.' The driver tapped the maid's shoulder and pointed to Ness. 'Could you tell me who this is?'

The maid looked at Ness and shook her head.

'This is ridiculous. Of course she doesn't know me,' Ness said. 'She's new, barely the same age as me.'

'Ridiculous, is it?' the driver snarled and grabbed her wrist.

Instinctively, Ness gave him a sharp punch to the nose. Swearing, the driver released her, staggering back. Ness turned to run but saw an elderly man striding over the rubble towards them. Although smudged with ash and cinders, she could see that his tails and striped trousers were those of a butler. A silver chain stretched across his bulging waistcoat.

'Rowson,' Ness called with relief as the butler drew close. 'Thank goodness.'

But the butler showed no sign of recognition.

'This girl reckons she lives 'ere,' said the driver, gripping his bleeding nose. 'She says she's Miss Bonehill.'

'That's impossible,' Rowson said, frowning at the driver and Ness. The butler's thinning grey hair fluttered in the breeze like the smoke that drifted across the ruins. 'Necessity Bonehill is dead. She has been these last five years. I went to her funeral myself.'

Better an honest enemy than a false friend.

Traditional proverb

CHAPTER EIGHT
BACK FROM THE GRAVE

Silence fell across the smoking ruins of Bonehill House as Ness tried to take in what Rowson had just said.

'Rowson, it's me, Necessity. I've been at Rookery Heights Academy for Young Ladies for the last five years!'

'I'm not sure who you are, miss,' Rowson said, stiffening. 'And I don't know if this is some kind of practical joke but it's in very poor taste considering the circumstances.'

'I knew it.' The driver gave a yellow grin in spite of his bleeding nose. 'Call a constable. She's barmy!'

Ness lurched forward, gripping Rowson's lapels. 'Please, Rowson. It's me, Ness. I used to lock Cook in the pantry and ride on the dumb waiter . . .'

Rowson frowned.

Is that recognition in his eyes?

His face hardened. 'I'm sorry, miss, but I'll not stand by and sully the memory of a poor, departed young girl. You do look familiar but you could be any one of thirty chambermaids dismissed in the last five years just chancing their arm.'

'But I *am* Necessity!' she pleaded.

Rowson slapped her hands away from him. 'Necessity Bonehill died of a fever contracted at Rookery Heights.' His voice rose to a bellow. 'I helped carry the coffin myself.'

'Police! Police!' the driver yelled. 'Mad girl on the loose!'

One of the urchins, seeing his chance to get rid of Ness, hurried off yelling, 'Murder!'

Ness glanced from the distant boy back to Rowson and the driver, who made a grab for her. She easily sidestepped it and sent him sprawling on to a pile of bricks.

'Rowson, surely you must remember – you always used to rescue me from Cook and Miss Cheem the governess –'

'Just go.' Rowson glared at Ness. Was it her imagination or were those tears glistening in his eyes? Then he whispered, 'Get out of here. It's not safe. The master and mistress weren't found in the wreckage. You must find them!'

Ness frowned. 'But where should I look? I don't know where to go.'

Rowson glanced down at the groaning driver and then looked at Ness again. 'Just run,' he said, his eyes beseeching. *He does recognise me!* 'Henry Lumm,' he whispered urgently. 'Gladwell Gardens. He can help you. Now go!'

A distant whistle accompanied shouts as the urchins came bounding over the rubble towards Ness. 'There she is,' called one boy.

'She's laid that cabby low,' called another.

The shrill police whistle grew louder.

Ness gave a cry of frustration, stuffed the satchel into the sack and sprinted off through the wreckage.

'Stop 'er,' the driver called.

A large man loomed from behind a column of blackened brick, opening his arms. Tucking the sack under her arm, Ness threw herself to the left, scraping along the brickwork and rolling under his right arm. She kicked into his calf muscle, sending him thumping to the ground.

Advancing deeper into the wreckage, she scurried around gutted rooms, glimpsing half-familiar sticks of furniture or scraps of fabric. All burned and singed. Suddenly, she was out of the ruins and in the small kitchen garden. A six-foot brick wall still sealed this area off. Ness glanced back. A mustachioed constable was gaining on her.

With a yell of defiance, she sprinted at the wall, bouncing on to a water barrel that stood against it and hurling herself upward. The top of the wall winded her as she landed there on her ribs. She dropped the sack over the other side but a strong hand gripped her ankle.

'Let go of me,' Ness snarled and kicked back, raking her heel down the side of the hand, aiming to cause more pain than damage.

'Ow! 'Ere, watch 'er – she's vicious,' the constable yelped as his grip loosened.

Ness swung her legs up and over the top of the wall.

She glanced round. She'd landed in a yard that backed on to another large house. She wasn't safe yet. She could hear voices echoing behind her but also to her left. A crowd was making its way round to the front of this house. Cursing under her breath, Ness snatched up the sack and sprinted to a small side gate. She slipped out of the yard and walked briskly down the street, trying to look casual.

'She's in the backyard there,' cried an urgent voice.

'Careful, she gave that copper a good old kick!' called one of the boys.

The end of the street drew near and she would be able to turn a corner and lose them any second. But the sound of hoofs on the cobbles made Ness groan. The hansom cab pulled level with her just before she reached the corner.

'Thought you'd managed to sneak off, did yer?' The driver leered. A bruise now ran across the bridge of his nose and blood caked one nostril.

Ness heaved a sigh, paused for a second and then approached the driver's seat.

'I should've done this in the first place,' she muttered.

Dropping the sack on the passenger seat, she quickly grabbed the driver's thumb, twisting it. He leaned forward, crying out. Ness dragged him down, pulled the whip from his other hand and planted him heavily head first on the cobbles.

Without looking back, she swung herself up into the driver's seat, gave a flick of the whip, a jig of the reins, and the horse skipped off, leaving the driver groaning on the ground.

The horse trotted on, weaving in and out of the other carriages and carts, taking her away from Bonehill House. Ness had driven traps before – with Morris – and the horse seemed to know where they were going. Once the ruins were well behind her, she relaxed a little. She tried to head for Gladwell Gardens but the horse had other ideas and trotted stubbornly eastward through ever-narrowing streets. The sack lay in her lap. Peering in, Ness saw charred papers and the elegant swirl of her mother's handwriting poking out of the satchel. A sob caught in her throat.

Ness sat numbly, allowing the horse to meander and barely noticing the stares and the occasional angry cry as the horse cut across another cab's path. Going back to her parents had been a chance to make everything all right. Instead things were much worse and more puzzling than she could ever have imagined. *Why did Mama and Father hide me in Rookery Heights and tell the world I had died?*

The horse stopped in a dingy back alley just outside the crumbling entrance to a courtyard. It had clearly made its way home. The windows in the sagging houses that lined the alley were cracked and grimy, but Ness could sense the peering eyes behind them. Perhaps the driver had made his way home too. No, surely he couldn't have arrived before her? Ness tried hard to think how long she'd been travelling.

She slid out of the seat and gave the horse a pat on the rump. With a whinny, it ambled into the courtyard while Ness hurried off up the narrow lane.

She had no sense of the real time in the twilight maze of streets. She didn't know where she was going either. Surely Jacob Carr would have set sail by now. Now there was no one to help her. Here and there, yells drifted from within the slums. Ragged, suspicious-eyed men smoking pipes watched her pass. She ignored the comments shouted after her.

The alleys seemed endless, running into stinking courtyards, splitting off into several directions. The stench of the river drifted up the dark passages. Ness wrinkled her nose at the green, slimy puddles that grey-faced children seemed happy to play in.

Footsteps echoed on the cobbles behind her, falling into rhythm with hers and speeding up as she increased her pace. Glancing over her shoulder, Ness saw three young men, unshaven, wearing crumpled top hats too big for them. Their clothes, although well made, were ill-fitting and patched. *Probably stolen*, Ness thought. The youth in the lead clenched a stubby clay pipe between his teeth as he grinned at her.

'Wait up, miss,' he called. 'We only want ter pass the time of day.'

Ness began to run, but the men were too close and soon caught up with her. One of them circled round in front, forcing Ness to stop.

'I wonder what you're doin' in these parts,' he grinned, his pipe waggling between his teeth. 'Harmy Sullivan,' he said, lifting his battered top hat to reveal a shock of shaggy, red hair.

'It ain't safe, a young lady without a chaperone this time o' day,' laughed another, darker-featured and smaller member of the gang, who nudged the lead man. 'Is it, Harmy?'

'It ain't safe any time o' day, Tulla.' Harmy nodded, looking Ness up and down. 'All kinds of ruffians roamin' these streets, up to no good.'

'We could chaperone 'er,' Tulla said, his voice theatrical as if he'd just thought of the idea and it came as a total surprise to him.

'No, thank you,' Ness said and turned to walk away.

More young men had appeared in front of her. There were at least eight of them now, grimy with city life, dressed in shabby grandeur.

'That's not nice. After me introducin' meself all genteel, like,' Harmy murmured. 'Surely you can spare some time to talk to us.'

Harmy made a grab for Ness's wrist but she brought it up to meet the bowl of his pipe, pushing it and its hot contents into his mouth. With a garbled scream of rage and agony, Harmy bent double trying to spit out the hot ash.

Ness charged forward, pulling one man's necktie and cracking his head against another's. But Tulla leapt forward too, swinging a stick at Ness. Its clubbed end clipped her head, sending her spinning to the cobbled ground.

The remaining five men advanced. Tulla slapped the stick into his palm with each step. In the background, Harmy Sullivan cursed and spat.

'I reckon you need teachin' a lesson, miss.' Tulla grinned. 'You have to show us a little respect.'

Ness shook her head, trying to clear her thoughts. Her temple pounded and blood trickled into her eye. With a well-aimed leg sweep, she could take two of them down, but the other three would still be ready to take their place. She tensed and prepared to spring.

Just then two men at the back crumpled to the ground as a screaming apparition appeared from above.

Ness recognised the boy in the turban at once. He was swinging two curved swords and howled like a lost soul. Two of the gang fled instantly, bowling Harmy over.

The boy hacked at Tulla, sweeping the broad blade at his head. Tulla screamed and fell to his knees, his top hat cut clean in half but no other damage done. The boy kicked out at him, sending him sprawling.

'Come with me quickly,' the boy snapped at Ness and set off at a brisk jog down a side alley.

Ness hesitated. Could she trust him?

Tulla groaned and began to pick himself up. 'Stop that bloomin' heathen,' Harmy yelled. He'd gathered his senses and was pulling one of the other gang members to his feet.

The boy paused and glared back at her. 'You must come now!' he hissed.

Ness took one glance at the quickly recovering gang and plunged after the boy in the turban.

THE AGED IN COUNCIL; THE YOUNG IN ACTION.

TRADITIONAL PROVERB

CHAPTER NINE

THE LASHKARS OF SULAYMAN

Ness panted, her old boots slapping on the cobbles. The boy's silhouette grew smaller as the distance between them opened up. He stopped and snapped, 'Hurry!' at her once and then darted down the alley. Left then right, then left again. Her head throbbed where Tulla had clipped her with the stick. She gritted her teeth, determined not to show any weakness to this stranger who had apparently rescued her. She had no idea where they were or where they were going. Ness felt as if she were doubling back on herself. Behind, angry voices still bounced around the courtyards and lanes of the slums. Soon she caught up with him.

The boy stopped so abruptly that Ness nearly ran into him. He squeezed between two barrels in an alcove and, to Ness's amazement, he disappeared. She followed and the alcove proved deeper than she had thought. It led through a short tunnel into a courtyard. A vivid blue gateway blocked their path at one end. It looked strange to Ness, curving to a point at the top. Arabic letters were inscribed around the frame of the gate. It reminded her of pictures of the sultan's palace in the *Arabian Nights* book she'd had at home.

The boy leaned close to the gate and knocked three times. Three knocks came back and he replied with one more, a pause and then a final knock. The gate swung open silently. The boy nodded Ness towards the opening. She hesitated but the shouts behind them had been growing louder.

'Hurry! They can't get in here,' the boy snarled. 'Unless you want to take your chances . . .'

'And I'm safe with you, who tried to kill me in the night?' Ness hissed back, putting a hand to her head. Blood coated her fingertips.

'I can explain. Just choose quickly because I'm not going to save you again.'

'Save me? You didn't –' Ness began, but the clatter of boots on the cobbles echoed down the passage. She stepped over the threshold and the gate crashed shut behind her.

Ness felt as if she had walked into another land. The marketplace that she stood in was whitewashed and clean, with a small fountain gurgling in the centre. Three alleys ran from each of the other sides. The square buzzed with activity. Turbaned men in smart suits squeezed past women in veils and brightly coloured dresses. Old ladies balanced baskets on their heads. Along one side, stalls leaned against each other, straining under the weight of rainbow-coloured piles of spices: rolls of material, silks and cottons, heaps of fruit and cages of chickens.

The boy grinned at her, then turned to a tall, bald man with a long, grey beard that reached to his round belly. He wore a black suit and had a scimitar tucked into his belt. They talked fast in a foreign language. Ness didn't understand but it was clear that the boy was relating their encounter with Harmy's gang.

'Suppose you tell me what's going on,' Ness said, narrowing her eyes at the boy.

He gave her a brief glance, made a final comment and then turned to her. 'My name is Azuli,' he said briskly. 'And this is Jabalah. He will take us to Hafid. He will explain everything.'

Azuli made to walk away but Jabalah bowed to Ness. 'A thousand welcomes to Arabesque Alley, miss,' he said, closing the gate. 'You are safe, rest assured. We should get that head wound attended to quickly.'

'Really, it's nothing,' Ness muttered, still stinging from Azuli's comment about saving her. She winced as Jabalah pressed a handkerchief to the wound and tied a makeshift bandage around her head.

'That should help,' he muttered. 'I will get my wife to treat it later. Now follow me.'

Ness nodded. Her head throbbed and a slight dizziness made everything seem even more distant and unreal. Jabalah reached to take the sack from her but Ness shrank back, hugging it to her. With a shrug, he turned and strode off. Ness followed and fell into step as Jabalah and Azuli pushed their way through the crowds. Jabalah limped slightly as he twisted and turned past people.

'Bet you never knew about this place?' Azuli grinned back at her as he led her through the narrow alleys. 'Few people do.'

Rounded windows with brightly coloured shutters dotted the walls and, now and then, Ness glimpsed courtyards with potted palms and fountains through doorways. She shook her head and ducked under a rug that dangled from the lines hanging overhead. Copper pots, baskets and food stalls lined the alleyway. True, it was alien to the London she knew, but something troubled her. She couldn't think what.

'We have lived here for nearly fifty years,' Jabalah said, 'but we keep our presence as quiet as possible.'

A mouth-watering smell filled the air, reminding her that she hadn't eaten since that morning and that so much had happened since then. Giving her a sidelong glance, Jabalah laughed, tore a chunk of flatbread from a nearby stall and handed it to Ness. He threw a coin to the stallholder.

'Hungry?' he said, smiling and patting his pot belly.

Ness bit into the bread, barely pausing to chew. Jabalah held up a finger to stop her biting into it again. Instead he took the remaining bread from her and dipped it into a nearby cooking pot. Ness took the bread, now coated in sweet-smelling gravy, and continued to devour it. It tasted divine. *Is it meat or fruit I can taste? It's definitely something sweet and yet . . .*

Jabalah grinned. 'It's good?'

'Delicious.' Ness smiled back and nodded. Then, recalling the previous night, she turned to Azuli. 'So why were you following me?' she snapped, her voice thick with bread and gravy. 'And why did you break into my dormitory and attack me in the middle of the night?'

Azuli's face became stern. 'Hafid will tell you what you need to know.'

They pushed on in silence. The crowd flowed past them, smiling and nodding. And then it struck her. *So many old people*, Ness thought. She glanced around. The crowd had grey hair and careworn faces. Their backs were bent under some heavy burden, something more than the sacks and baskets they carted around with them.

Jabalah stopped at another ornate door framed with tiles and flowing Arabic script. The courtyard beyond was decorated with symmetrical patterns that seemed to merge into one another. A palm grew in the corner of the yard. It was warm in there. Ness looked up to see that the yard had a glass roof. They passed through another doorway and clambered up several flights of stairs and through an entrance covered by a heavy curtain.

They stood in a large room, richly decorated with wall hangings and paintings. Ness's shoes slid on the tiled floor. Daylight flooded through two doors that opened on to a balcony.

An old man rocked to and fro on a backless low sofa in the centre of the room. He wore black robes but his bald head was uncovered. Ness shivered as he stared in her direction with blind, white eyes.

'We have brought the girl, Hafid,' Azuli said, bowing low to the old man.

'You are Necessity Bonehill?' Hafid said. His voice sounded cracked and stretched.

'Yes,' Ness replied, giving a slight curtsy in spite of herself. 'Forgive me, sir, but how do you know my name?'

Hafid gave a broad smile. 'It is only fair that you understand. Sit.' He pointed to a cushioned stool close to him. 'We are the Lashkars of Sulayman.'

Ness settled herself on the stool, glad to rest as her head still throbbed.

The ancient man raised himself up and began in a reedy voice. 'Once, Sulayman ruled justly over men, djinns and all animals. He could speak to the birds, such was the will of Allah.' The old man planted his palms on the floor and dragged himself towards Ness, his white eyes staring at her. 'But not all were happy to be ruled by Sulayman. The djinns, like man himself, have free will. They can choose to follow God or the devil. The djinns were a powerful race, full of magic and enchantment. Some were too proud to bow to a human king and they rebelled. An army of djinns rose up and lay waste to a third of Sulayman's kingdom.'

'Djinns?' Ness said breathlessly. The thing in her dream had called himself a djinn.

The wizened old man gave a croaking laugh. 'Creatures of fire and light. Beings of the most powerful magic. You might call them demons but they are more than that.' Hafid rocked back and forth and continued with his tale. 'With the help of Allah, Sulayman crushed the djinns. Those who would not repent were each trapped in a brass bottle sealed with powerful spells and plunged into the darkest chasms of the sea –'

'But mankind is ever curious and self-serving,' Azuli interrupted. 'Kings and magicians from the world over sought the bottles, hoping to harness the power inside.'

Hafid nodded and chuckled, sucking at his toothless gums. 'Sulayman created an order of holy warriors, or Lashkars, and set them to guard the place where the bottles lay. He charged them with ensuring that nobody ever disturbed the djinns inside.'

'But someone did disturb them?' Ness stared at the old man, spellbound by his story.

'Years passed, decades rolled on,' the old man said, his voice growing stronger. 'The Lashkars passed their holy duty on from father to son, but they became lazy. They thought their job easy and fell into ways of luxury and decadence. One night, an evil magician of immense power stole the bottles, hoping to open them and release chaos into the world. Only Sulayman's personal intervention stopped him but the bottles were then scattered across the four corners of the world. Lost.' Hafid looked forlorn. He licked his lips and leaned further forward. 'In his fury, Sulayman charged his Lashkars and all their descendants with finding every bottle and destroying the djinns inside. This we must do – or die trying.'

Hafid stared, lost in time, at the crows that crowded the balcony.

Jabalah gave an uncomfortable cough and continued for the old man. 'Only a silver sword carved with the djinn's name would kill it. Knowing this, Sulayman forged one such weapon for each missing djinn. When the djinn's blood was spilled, the blade would melt like ice in the summer sun.'

Silence fell over the room as Ness tried to take in this story.

Jabalah heaved a sigh. 'For almost three thousand years, the Lashkars of Sulayman have wandered the world, making for wherever a rumour of a bottle or a djinn sprang up. We have sacrificed everything for our holy duty. Wherever the merchants of the world met, there we would be. London has become the centre of the world, the hub of a huge empire. All news and rumours pass through here, so this has become our most permanent home. We are the last of the Lashkars. We have one silver sword left. There is only one djinn remaining.'

'You unleashed it, Necessity Bonehill,' croaked the old man, returning to them. 'And you will be our key to finding and destroying it.'

GREAT SOULS HAVE WILLS; FEEBLE ONES ONLY HAVE WISHES.

TRADITIONAL PROVERB

CHAPTER TEN
HOME TRUTHS

Ness stared dumbfounded at Hafid. 'This is madness,' she said, glowering at the men around her. 'Djinns and Sulayman? The truth is that you've kidnapped my parents and now you want money for it, but you had to get me out of the way first. That's right, isn't it?'

Hafid sighed. 'No, my child. Your father started all this many years ago – we suspect that the bottle came into his possession before you were even born – and we've been watching your family ever since. But we have been powerless to influence events until now.'

'Your father,' Jabalah muttered, 'unleashed the djinn some thirteen years ago, but then managed to return him to the bottle somehow. No mean feat. By the time we'd tracked him down, the bottle was gone. He denied all knowledge of it.'

'He nearly destroyed us,' Hafid said, shaking his head. 'He has friends in high places – he set the police on us, and when they'd finished his personal thugs tried to frighten us off too. He is a dangerous man to cross, your father.'

Ness thought of her father. Was he capable of such cruelty? She shook her head. 'This is too much. I won't believe it.'

'Azuli was trying to retrieve the bottle before *you* opened it,' Jabalah said, putting a protective arm around the boy's shoulder.

'I saw the man with a strange package at Rookery Heights and guessed what it was. I would have got it that night but you awoke,' Azuli muttered, giving her a dark look. 'And I had to flee.'

'The fact of the matter is that first your father and now you have opened the bottle, Miss Bonehill,' Hafid said, sounding like a hanging judge. 'The djinn is loose and it is our sworn duty to destroy him. You will assist us.'

'This is ridiculous,' Ness exclaimed, reddening as all eyes fell on her. 'I can't help you.' Panic and anger swirled in Ness's stomach. These men were propelling her into something she knew nothing about and wasn't sure she even believed in. It was insane!

Hafid narrowed his eyes again. 'I think you can, Necessity Bonehill,' he whispered. 'I sense that you are important to our quest. You aren't like others . . . Do you feel that?'

Ness's cheeks reddened even more. 'I don't know what you mean,' she lied. Of course she felt different. She always had. She wasn't like the silly girls at the Academy – or like anyone for that matter. She was a Bonehill. She was special!

'Before we can take the silver blade into battle,' Hafid said, sucking on his toothless gums, 'we must locate the djinn.'

'And then who will carry the final sword?' a voice called from the door.

Ness turned to see another tall, old man, his silver hair emphasised by the darkness of his skin. Ness could tell he had once been a fighter by his poise and grace but he had thinned with age. He wore rich silk robes of purple and a red turban with a jewelled clasp at the front.

'Father,' Azuli said, hurrying to his open arms.

Ness felt a sting of jealousy as father embraced son. Although they both had fierce, glittering eyes, Azuli did not share Taimur's sharp, hawkish nose.

'I will carry the sword. Taimur, you know I am younger than you,' Jabalah said, worry lining his face. 'That honour should fall to me.'

Ness looked from one man to the next. They all looked ancient to her. Something troubled her. The same feeling she had had as Jabalah led her through the streets. As if she were looking at a picture and some obvious detail was missing. *What is it?*

'No, you fought the previous djinn,' Taimur said, ruffling his son's hair. 'I am senior. I should carry the sword.'

'Father, no!' Azuli stepped back. 'You can't!' He turned to Hafid and dropped to his knees. 'Hafid, with the greatest respect, the Lashkars are old. The tragedies of the years have ravaged them. Give me the chance to lay the final djinn to rest!'

'You do not lack courage, Azuli,' Hafid muttered, shaking his head. 'But you are not truly of our line. An adopted child never inherits the Lashkar blood.'

Azuli stood up. 'I'm not good enough? Is that what you're saying?'

'Azuli!' Taimur snapped, grabbing his son's shoulder.

Hafid swayed as if Azuli's outburst would blow him down. 'It is not a question of whether you are good enough. It is whether or not you understand our true calling. You are rash and impetuous. Nobody asked you to steal the bottle, yet you tried. And you failed.'

Azuli stood fuming but unable to counter the accusation.

'I've heard enough –' Ness began.

'The djinn is free,' Hafid hissed, grabbing her wrist with his withered hand. Ness could see the veins pulsing within, the bony knuckles and cracked nails. 'I can smell his foul breath on the wind of the city. You know it's true!'

'Let go and find him then!' Ness cried, snatching her arm from his grasp. 'I saw a creature, smoke and then . . . the girls at the Academy, they . . . It was horrible . . . Now he has my parents too. And it's all my fault.'

'To find the djinn, we must think first, then act. Tell me, Miss Bonehill, why did you open the bottle?' Hafid said, leaning forward in his seat.

'I didn't know what was in it,' Ness sniffed, hugging the sack to her. 'It was sent to me by Uncle Carlos.'

'Carlos Grossford,' murmured Taimur.

'You know him?' Ness gasped, staring at the stern-looking man.

'Knew him,' Hafid said softly and inclined his head. 'He was murdered last month . . . his throat cut.'

'Murdered? Last month?' Ness's eyes widened, her heart pounded. Tears stung her eyes. *Poor Uncle Carlos*. 'But he only sent me the bottle a few days ago. Why would anyone want to . . . ?'

'Why *wouldn't* anyone?' Taimur said, giving a snort. 'Grossford was involved in all manner of extortion.'

'No.' Ness shook her head. She gasped for breath. All this talk of djinns and murder was too incredible.

'You have the bottle now?' Hafid whispered.

Ness nodded. Hafid extended his scrawny hand and, slowly, Ness handed it over. Hafid pulled the bottle out of the sack, his breath hissing between his teeth as he ran his fingers over the hideous patterns around its sides. He placed it on the floor in front of him. For a moment, they all stood in silence, staring at the bottle.

'It's horrible,' Azuli whispered, kneeling down and running a fingertip down the neck.

'What is horrible is the fact that it is open and empty,' Taimur growled, staring coldly at Ness.

'So did he offer you a wish?' Hafid said, his milky eyes holding Ness.

'He did,' Ness said, glaring at the old man, daring him to question further.

'What did you ask for?' Hafid said quietly.

'I can't say.' Ness flushed with shame. She couldn't tell these complete strangers that she'd wished that her parents loved her. 'But the djinn said it would be granted in seven days and that it would cost me everything.'

'Seven days,' Hafid murmured. 'Then we don't have much time if you are to help us.'

'I just want to save my parents,' Ness said, sniffling.

Taimur gave a snort of impatience. 'How can we even trust her? She is a Bonehill! It wouldn't surprise me if this were all an elaborate plan to destroy us!'

'That does it,' Ness snapped, jumping to her feet. 'I don't know about this djinn or Lashkars or any of your mumbo-jumbo, but I'm not going to sit here while you call me a liar, Uncle Carlos a blackmailer and my father a bully and . . . and worse.'

Hafid silenced them both with a wave of his hand.

'Although you have not proven yourself to be deceptive yet, the rest are, sadly, truths, young lady,' Hafid said, shaking his head. 'We want the djinn and the djinn has your parents. We must work together.'

'I will go to my father's friend, Mr Henry Lumm,' Ness said, glaring at Taimur. 'He'll know what to do.'

'And this Lumm will help you? Ha! We have fought djinns for generations,' Taimur muttered. 'What could he possibly do?'

'Miss Bonehill,' Jabalah said, bowing and casting an irritated glance at Taimur, 'please, it is growing dark and you do not have anywhere to go. At least accept our hospitality for one night.'

Ness looked from man to man. They were right. She didn't even have the first idea how to get to Gladwell

Gardens from this part of London – but she couldn't tell them that. 'Very well, I will stay tonight, but in the morning I'm going to Henry Lumm,' she said stubbornly.

'If it is acceptable, my wife and I will accommodate Miss Bonehill,' Jabalah said to Hafid, who nodded in agreement.

Ness followed the tall warrior out of the room. She could hear the muttering beginning as soon as the curtain swished back across the doorway.

They strode silently through the streets. People were closing up their stalls and houses as night drew on. Finally they came to a row of well-kept whitewashed tenements. Jabalah stopped at one of the houses. A grey-haired woman in scarlet robes that covered her head met them at the door. Ness could tell that in her youth the woman would have been a great beauty. Even now, age hadn't stooped her back or wrinkled her skin.

'Necessity, this is Suha, my wonderful wife.' Jabalah flashed a huge white-toothed grin and put an arm around Suha. Ness curtsied and Suha bowed, giving a little laugh.

'You are very welcome,' she said to Ness and beckoned for her to sit down. Suha gestured to Jabalah. 'There is some fruit in the kitchen,' she said. 'Necessity will be hungry.'

Ness felt the tension flow from her as she settled on to the cushioned divan. Soon the big man returned with a bowl of fruit. She glanced around the room. Jabalah's home proved to be less sumptuous than Hafid's. Wall hangings adorned the main room, with a divan and a few cushions scattered about. Through the rounded doorway Ness could see an adjoining bedroom and a small kitchen. On a table by the hearth was a small portrait of a young man dressed in the black garb of the Lashkars. He looked very proud and handsome brandishing his scimitar.

Suha followed her gaze and gave a sigh.

'My son,' she said, with a sad smile. 'He is with Allah now.'

'I'm sorry,' Ness said, looking down at her hands.

'It was some time ago.' Suha smiled softly, walking over to the table and picking up the picture. 'We lost him while fighting a djinn. Him and so many others.' She gently replaced the picture and busied herself arranging a bed for Ness.

That night Ness lay on a makeshift bed of cushions, listening to murmured conversation from Jabalah and Suha's room. Suha had bathed her wounds and put a clean dressing on her head. Ness glanced down at the satchel by her side. She lifted the scorched flap and inched out the fragile leaves of paper. The smell of ash tickled her nose, reminding her of the charred ruin that had been her home. Most of the sheets were blackened and they flaked apart at her touch, but some more central ones were less damaged. Ness peered at the brown paper and gave a gasp. *My name*, she thought. *It's a letter. A letter for me.*

My dearest Necessity, I know you will never read this letter, nor the many hundred letters I have written before. I thought of posting them. Oh! How I dreamt of you receiving just one letter and knowing why I sent you . . .

Tears blurred Ness's vision. Singe marks ate into the paper, censoring whole paragraphs, giving her random morsels of sentences.

I married for love . . .

The fire had left tantalising fragments.

I fear your father . . . I long for the day we can be free . . . I never wanted . . . I wish . . .

The paper crackled and snapped in her shaking grip.

My darling child, one day you'll understand . . .

Tears coursed, hot, down her cheek, salting her lips as she read the final vanishing words.

I will always love you.

So why send me away? thought Ness. Falling on to her pillow, she sobbed herself into a fitful sleep.

In her dreams, Ness wandered the rooms of Bonehill House, a small child once more. The sunlit drawing room where her mother would sing her nursery rhymes, her room where she read bedtime stories, her father's study where the bloodstone ring lay . . .

Ness snapped her eyes open and sat up. She heard Suha's soft weeping in the next room. A mother crying for her lost son. A mother who cared. Was her own mother crying for her somewhere?

She lay down again and squeezed her eyes shut. The bloodstone ring sat on Father's desk. It was the one thing in the study he let her play with. Why think of it now?

'Take it, my Necessity,' he used to say, grinning like the sly old fox in her stories. 'Try it on. See its beauty, the deep red fire that glows within each vein?'

It was the one time she had seen her mother stand up to her father.

'Anthony, don't,' she had snapped. 'She's not one of your experiments!'

'Isn't she?' her father had said and laughed. Not an easy laugh, full of good humour, but a harsh laugh that haunted Ness's dreams all night.

Better do it than wish it done.

Traditional proverb

CHAPTER ELEVEN
HENRY LUMM

With a lurch of her stomach, Ness woke abruptly. She stared around the room, trying to make sense of the scattered cushions, the strange-looking furniture. Then she remembered where she was. Relief flooded through her.

'You managed to sleep.' Suha came into the room, carrying a tray of flatbread and fruit.

Ness smiled and nodded. 'Not at first but I must have drifted off eventually. What time is it?'

'It's mid-morning.' Suha smiled. 'You must have been exhausted after all you've been through.'

'I was,' Ness agreed, biting into a slab of bread.

So much had happened, it was overwhelming. Why had the djinn taken her parents? Her parents . . . Ness hardly recognised them from the Lashkars' description. And how could she stop the djinn? This was the second day. Five more and the djinn would come for her and then what? Ness shivered. Whatever happened, it would cost her everything.

'You are full of dark brooding.' Suha sighed. 'Do you miss your parents?'

'I don't know,' Ness murmured, chewing slowly. She tried to picture them. Her father proud and well dressed, black hair slicked back, eyes cold and blue. Her mother slim and anxious, her blonde hair pinned up, her lips pressed together. That was how Ness had always imagined them, as if sitting for a portrait. Ness shook her head. 'I hardly know my parents.'

'That is a great shame.' Suha gave a sad smile and sat down next to Ness. 'Children should be enjoyed and treasured. So soon do they grow up, so easily are they lost.'

Ness remembered Suha weeping in the night. 'Have the Lashkars lost many children?' Ness wondered aloud, immediately regretting her thoughtless question.

Suha nodded slowly. 'Many, over the years,' she said. 'Our people are raised to fight against almost impossible odds and the last djinn we defeated cursed us in such a cruel way.'

'He cursed the Lashkars?' Ness gasped.

'With his dying breath,' Suha said, putting a hand to her mouth. 'He banished our children and grandchildren. Every man, woman, child and babe in arms.'

'Banished them?' Ness said, stroking Suha's arm. 'Where to?'

Suha shook her head. 'Nobody knows,' she sighed. 'The djinn perished saying that our future generations would suffer as the djinn had but they simply vanished. Hafid believes they are trapped somewhere, in a vessel or something similar. Now only the grandparents are left.'

There are no children! That's what I noticed yesterday in Arabesque Alley, Ness thought. *Apart from . . .*

Azuli appeared at the arched doorway, looking sullen. Suha stifled her tears and wiped her face, stepping back from Ness, who glared at the boy for his rude intrusion.

'Hafid says I must escort you to this Lumm fellow's place. He says it is a good place to start,' he muttered. 'Jabalah will meet us at the gate. I will go with you.'

'I didn't ask for an escort,' Ness snapped. 'I don't need one. Just tell me how to get to Lumm's house.'

'My orders are to accompany you,' Azuli snarled back.

'Here,' Suha said, handing Ness a sack. 'Some food for later, just in case.'

'Thank you, Suha,' she said, trying to sound grateful and to glare at Azuli at the same time.

Ness followed Azuli through the narrow streets of Arabesque Alley. Passers-by eyed her nervously. Some shook their heads.

'Rumours spread faster than fever,' Azuli murmured. 'They know what you have done. We have made some enquiries and your Mr Lumm lives in Gladwell Gardens.'

'I know,' Ness muttered. 'I told you, I don't need your help.'

'So you keep saying,' Azuli said, pushing open the blue gate to the outside world. 'But we're not giving you a choice.'

'Nobody's asking you to follow me,' Ness yelled, balling her fists and stamping her feet.

Azuli's dark eyes flashed and his nostrils flared, making him look even more like his proud father. 'Do you think I want to follow you? You're impossible! I wish you *could* lose me in the crowd, then I could get on with the proper business at hand – killing the djinn – instead of nurse-maiding –'

Ness flicked her forearm forward, delivering a stunning blow to Azuli's chin. He staggered backward through the gate and fell flat on his back.

'Wish granted,' Ness snorted, before turning on her heel and striding off.

She glanced up and down the murky alleyway outside the gate, expecting at any moment to bump into Harmy Sullivan and his hooligan friends. The day before, Ness had hardly taken in the twists and turns of the alleys as she had followed Azuli but she seemed to know instinctively which way to go.

She emerged on to a busy street. The brightness and bustle dazzled her after the dank closeness of the alley-ways. Street sellers of all kinds called out their wares as people pushed past them. Carriages rattled across the cobbles. Someone yelled at a careless pedestrian who had nearly stepped out in front of a cab. Ness's heart sank. London was so big and busy. She didn't have the first idea where Gladwell Gardens were. It was all very well know-ing an address, but another thing altogether trying to find it.

She leaned against a shop window, watching all of London life pass by. She could hear her father's voice echoing in her head.

'The common herd,' he used to say. 'Remember, Necessity, you are better than them. You are my daughter. Mine.'

'You are special,' her mother had told her repeatedly.

Then why dump me in the Academy and pretend that I died? she thought bitterly.

A sudden movement caught Ness's eye. Azuli stood only a few feet away from her, glancing around and scratching his head. He winced and put a hand to his bruised chin, making her smirk. He turned and stared right through her. Ness ducked into the crowd but Azuli still stood perplexed, scanning the passers-by for any sign of her.

He must have seen me, she thought, hurrying along the street. *He looked right at me*.

Something clinked in her sack as she bustled through the crowd. She stopped and frowned, opening it. A few pennies lay nestled next to the slab of bread Suha had put in. Ness shook her head. She didn't think Jabalah or Suha could afford to give away money but she could hardly refuse it. *Why are they so generous when they're clearly so poor?* Ness wondered. *I'll repay them when I find Mama and Father*.

Checking the drivers closely, Ness approached a cab stand and soon found herself rattling towards Gladwell Gardens.

*

Henry Lumm's house was grand and imposing. Black railings stood as sharp sentries along the front of the white stone building. The windows frowned out at Ness, daring her to set one foot on the steps that swept up to the shiny, black front door. Ness glanced around her. Her grubby skirt and stained jacket stood out in this street full of smart carriages and silken-clad ladies twirling parasols against the feeble spring sunshine.

Lumm was a friend of her father's but Ness had no real memories of him. Now she stood at his front door about to throw herself on his mercy. Would he even believe her? What if he thought she was dead too? Ness drew a deep breath. There was nothing for it but to knock.

Clambering up the steps, Ness paused. The front door stood slightly ajar. Perhaps the last visitor had forgotten to shut it on their way out.

'Hello?' she called, pushing on the heavy door. It creaked ominously, making Ness catch her breath.

The smell of polish and the ticking of a huge grandfather clock reassured Ness as she poked her head around the door. Her boots clicked on the woodblock floor as she glanced about. Doors stood to her left and right. A richly carpeted stairway led up into a shadowy landing. The hall lay deserted but a brass bell sat on a squat mahogany table. Stepping in, Ness closed the door behind her and rang the bell.

The ring sounded shrill and far too loud in the quiet house, making her wince. She waited, twisting her fingers nervously. *Where is everyone?* Surely Henry Lumm would have an army of staff, judging by his house. Ness wanted to call out again but the thought of her voice drifting up into the seemingly empty house stopped her. She pushed open the side door to her left and peered into the room.

It was a study of some kind. Books lined the shelves and a huge globe stood in the middle of the room. With a jolt, she realised that a figure sat with their back to Ness.

'Excuse me,' Ness began as she edged over to the figure. 'I'm sorry for the intrusion but the door was open.'

The figure didn't turn around. Ness could see a shiny scalp through thinning grey hair as she approached.

She spoke again. 'I hope you don't mind. I was looking for . . .'

Ness couldn't finish her sentence. The sight of the chair's occupant stole the words from her mouth. A burly man with a walrus moustache sat staring into space. His skin was grey, the rims of his eyes red. A look of sheer terror twisted his face and a single line of blood trickled from the corner of his mouth.

There was no doubt in Ness's mind that Henry Lumm was dead and that he had met a violent end.

Because we kept an eye on the snake, we forgot the scorpion.

Traditional proverb

CHAPTER TWELVE

WHISPERS OF THE DEAD

One hand still held a pen. Ink leeched into the blotter on which it rested and pooled across the lacquered surface of the desk.

Ness felt cold, her heart thundered against her ribs. *I should get help*, she thought, but she stood immobile, her hands clutched together.

Her eyes were drawn to a half-written letter that lay pinned under Henry Lumm's other hand.

My dearest Olwen,

I fear our past has caught up with us. Grossford is dead. Bonehill and his wife are missing. The fiend is out, I'm sure of it. Hide yourself. Use whatever defences you have. Be certain that he will come for us all . . .

Ness's head pounded. *The fiend? Did he mean the djinn?* An envelope lay next to the letter with an address.

> *Mrs Olwen Quilfy, 4 Badenock Terrace, Kensington, London.*

With a grimace, Ness snatched up the letter and envelope. Maybe this Quilfy woman would have some answers. She clearly knew something more than Ness did. Ness turned to go but stopped. *I can't just leave*, she thought, glancing back at Lumm. Every fibre of her body wanted to run headlong out of the house but surely the alarm should be raised.

The house lay silent. Was there anyone about? Ness tiptoed out across the hall and clambered up the first few steps of the staircase.

'Hello?' she called to the rooms upstairs. Her voice sounded weak and her throat felt dry. 'Is there anybody there?'

Nothing.

Ness bit her lip. She glanced down the hall to where a door stood ajar. Steps led down to the kitchen. The smell of carbolic soap and cooking replaced the polish and cigar smoke of the upper floor as Ness descended the whitewashed steps.

She peered into the scrubbed kitchen. A tap dripped, the sound deafening in the quiet. The small room looked unremarkable, with its red tiled floor, a sink and a blacked range built into the chimney breast. But a woman lay collapsed over the bleached wooden table. She wore an apron and mob cap, clearly the cook. Ness gave a gasp. The woman's red-rimmed eyes stared blankly across the room. She was dead. Boils covered her skin. Her hair hung down under the cap, plastered to her blue-tinged face.

Glancing over her shoulder, Ness could see another body sprawled across the floor into the tiny pantry. A striped trouser leg and shiny boot told her it was a butler or footman of some description. She glimpsed more ulcerated flesh.

Images of Mollie, Sarah and Hannah gasping for breath fought their way into Ness's mind. She remembered them wheezing as the sweat drenched their nightclothes. Shaking her head, Ness stumbled back out of the kitchen. No one in this house could help her. She turned and scurried up the steps, her feet sounding like thunder in the deathly hush.

A crash from the kitchen below brought Ness skidding to a halt on the cool tiles of the hall. At the same time a movement from Lumm's study caught her eye. Something had lurched from her field of vision.

Lumm's chair was empty. A shadow shifted from behind the half-closed door.

With a cry, Ness threw herself at the front door. Her fingers felt like rubber as she fumbled at the door latch.

A long, groaning breath hissed out of Lumm's study followed by a heavy footfall. Below, a chair scraped across the tiles as if someone was standing up.

She freed the latch and the door swung open. Ness gave a gasp as the cool air outside struck her. But everything began to blur and fade into blackness. Azuli's face swam before her. A flash of flame dazzled her eyes and then she felt weightless and knew nothing more.

Darkness crushed in on Ness. It made no difference whether her eyes were open or closed. She tried to reach out into the black void that surrounded her but her arms were pinned by her sides. It felt like a band of metal constricted her limbs and body. An icy cold seeped into the marrow of her bones.

'Imagine,' a voice whispered in her ear, 'being trapped like this for a week.' It was the djinn's voice.

Ness's heart pounded. She wriggled and twisted but could not move an inch.

'Where are you?' Ness cried out. 'Let me see you.'

'Imagine being trapped for a month. A year. A hundred years. A thousand!' the djinn hissed. 'Sealed for ever in a cold metal tomb. Why? Because I didn't bend my knee to the tyrant Sulayman.'

'What's that got to do with me? Where are my parents? Why are you doing this?' Ness's voice screamed into the pitch black.

'They are safe. For now. Do you think your parents love you yet?' the djinn mocked her.

'I . . . don't know,' Ness muttered.

'Do you love them?' the djinn sneered.

'I'm not sure,' Ness hissed. 'Why do you take so much pleasure in tormenting me?'

'Because it's what I'm used to, Necessity,' the djinn replied. 'I think you do love your parents. Why else would you rush all over London looking for them? That's going to make it so hard. At the end, I mean.'

'I don't understand,' Ness wailed.

'Do you really think those Lashkars can help you find them? A bunch of decrepit old men? Beware of them, Necessity,' the djinn said, ignoring her comment.

'Why don't you just leave me alone?' Ness sobbed.

'Now *that* would have been a half-decent wish,' the djinn cackled. 'But you wanted your parents to love you instead. You have, I believe, five days left.'

The djinn's laughter rang in Ness's ears as she tried unsuccessfully to kick out at the darkness that enveloped her. She tossed and turned, her body becoming freer, light seeping into her vision. Gradually the hard metal casing that surrounded her softened and became more yielding until she felt bedclothes wrapping her.

With a start she sat up. Ness was in Suha's room.

Suha sat staring from the side of the bed, her hands holding Ness's shoulders. 'It is all right,' she said. 'You are safe.'

Ness fell back on to her pillows and blew out a sigh of relief. 'I dreamt of the djinn, of being trapped in a bottle. It was so real.'

Suha smoothed the hair from Ness's face. 'It was only a dream. You are safe now,' she said. 'You gave Azuli the slip but he knew where you were going. A good thing too, by the sounds of it. Azuli saved you. Another minute and you would have been . . .' Suha looked away and shook her head.

'Would have been what?' Ness asked, frowning.

'The djinn's strength is growing,' Suha murmured, avoiding Ness's gaze. 'It brings a deadly plague.'

'A plague?' Ness whispered, thinking of the girls at the Academy and the servants at Lumm's house.

'Death comes quickly but painfully,' Suha said. 'But it is more than just a plague. Once the poor souls have perished from the disease, their bodies become the instruments of the djinn. They rise again as his slaves. We Lashkars call them Pestilents.'

Ness threw her hand to her mouth. 'Lumm moved from his seat while I was there,' she gasped. 'But he was dead. I saw him with my own eyes.'

'He has become a Pestilent then,' Suha sighed, shaking her head. 'A living dead thing mindlessly following the djinn's commands.'

'That's horrible,' Ness whispered. 'This djinn must be truly evil to use people so.'

'Thankfully Azuli got you away in time,' Suha said, giving a tight smile.

'He won't let me forget that in a hurry,' Ness muttered, rubbing her eyes. She should be grateful but instead her stomach churned and she gritted her teeth. Why couldn't it have been Jabalah or one of the older Lashkars? 'Where is he now?'

'Azuli was taken to Hafid almost as soon as he arrived back with you. They have been arguing ever since.'

'About the djinn?'

'About that, and you,' Suha said.

'Me?'

'About what to do with you.'

A feeble tapping on the door stopped Ness from questioning Suha further. Hafid leaned against the door frame, wheezing as if the effort of standing was too much, let alone moving. He stared blindly into the room. *How does he find his way around?* Ness wondered.

'Forgive my intrusion,' he said in his thin reedy voice. 'We require your presence, Miss Bonehill. We must decide the best course of action.'

'I've told you I must find my parents,' Ness said with frustration. 'I haven't time to talk.'

'I think you'll find that you have no choice,' Hafid sighed and shook his head. 'And as for searching for your parents, you won't be going anywhere.'

WAIT FOR LUCK AND WAIT FOR DEATH.

TRADITIONAL PROVERB

CHAPTER THIRTEEN
BAIT IN A TRAP

'What do you mean, not going anywhere?' Ness glared at Hafid.

'If you come now then you will find out.' Hafid looked sombre and Ness gave a growl of indignation as she clambered off the bed. Hafid tilted his head towards Ness, listening to her movements. 'You rise quickly for one who has had such a shock, Miss Bonehill.'

'I feel much better,' Ness admitted. It was true – apart from a slightly stiff neck she felt fine.

'Then you will be well enough to present your concerns personally,' Hafid murmured.

Ness pulled on her old jacket and followed Hafid as he shuffled out into the alleyways.

'A new day,' Ness muttered to herself. *The third day. Four more to go until I lose everything. But what have I got left to lose?*

The business of Arabesque Alley continued as normal, people bustling to and fro, street vendors crying their wares, except these weren't the apples and vegetables or flowers and goods that were sold elsewhere in London. Ness could smell spices and incense; she could see curiously shaped fruit and brilliantly coloured cloth. She marvelled at how quickly Hafid moved considering his lack of sight.

'I've known these streets for decades,' Hafid said, as if reading her mind. 'You don't always need eyes to see where you're going.'

'I can't believe that the Lashkars have been here for all this time and nobody knows,' Ness said, weaving her way through the crowd after Hafid.

The old man paused but didn't look back at her. 'Some people know we are here. We cause them no problem, they ignore us. If you aren't looking for something then you aren't likely to find it. And Arabesque Alley isn't somewhere you stumble across. I make sure of that.' He tapped the side of his curved nose and gave a sly grin.

Ness stared after the old man. 'Are you some kind of magician?' she said.

Hafid stopped again. 'Some may call me that but what I can do is nothing compared to the power of the djinn. I have but a small fraction of the wisdom and gifts Sulayman commanded – charms, minor enchantments. They keep us safe.'

They came to another whitewashed tenement. Hafid grunted as he clambered up the steps and pushed the door open.

Inside, Taimur stood glowering and his fury was mirrored in the eyes of Azuli next to him. Jabalah sat on a heavily cushioned sofa at the side of the room. He gave Ness a brief smile and glanced sidelong at Hafid as the old man slumped beside him.

'So, Necessity Bonehill,' Taimur said, 'once more, you stumble into danger and Azuli has to pull you clear.'

Ness pursed her lips and stared at her feet.

'My son risked his life against the Pestilents that the djinn left to finish Miss Bonehill off and he doesn't even get a word of thanks?' Taimur almost spat.

'I didn't ask him to follow me,' Ness snapped back, staring Taimur in the eye. 'I can look after myself.'

'Ha!' Taimur laughed. 'Another moment and you would have joined Lumm, a mindless dead thing spreading contagion in the streets.'

'We took care of that, Father,' Azuli said, laying a hand on his arm.

'Took care?' Ness felt light-headed.

'We burned the house down,' Azuli said darkly. 'And all those inside it.'

'Lord above.' Ness sat down heavily.

'This isn't some game we are playing,' Taimur hissed through clenched teeth.

'This is our solemn duty, Necessity,' Jabalah said, his face etched with regret. 'We must protect mankind from the djinn regardless of the cost. We cannot afford to take any chances.'

'They were all dead at Gladwell Gardens long before you arrived,' Hafid said softly. 'The fire will slow the contagion. But every hour that the djinn is free is another hour for his poison to spread through the veins of this city.'

'Then we must find him quickly,' Azuli cried, slapping his fist into his palm. 'Take the silver blade to him.'

'As I said, we must think first,' Hafid said, his voice rising, 'then act.' He rubbed his long fingers over his wrinkled face. 'Why would the djinn kill Lumm? It doesn't make sense. Unless . . .' He balled his hands into fists and cracked his joints, deep in thought. 'How many wishes did the djinn offer you, Miss Bonehill?'

'Just one,' Ness said, trying to follow Hafid's train of thought. 'And then he said he would return for me in seven days.'

'Djinns are bound by the spell that traps them,' Hafid muttered. 'He had to offer at least one wish and then he'd be free. Yet we are sure that your father unleashed the djinn *and* succeeded in returning him to the bottle.'

'How is that possible,' Jabalah said, scratching his bald head, 'unless he wished the djinn straight back into the bottle?'

'I do not know,' Hafid said, shaking his head. 'It seems unlikely that Bonehill made such a wish because he came into great wealth soon after the time we think he released the creature.'

'My father has always been wealthy,' Ness snapped, frowning.

Jabalah gave an apologetic smile and shook his head. 'Your father was a poor army captain in the

Hinderton Rifles fourteen years ago. He married a rich heiress.'

'The Hinderton Rifles?' Ness repeated. *Sergeant Major Morris's regiment. Do Major Morris and Father know each other?*

'Your mother's parents disowned their daughter for marrying a man with so few prospects,' Jabalah said, his voice soft. He looked at the floor. 'But within eighteen months, her parents were dead, your mother inherited everything and you were born. Bonehill was quite the respectable gentleman all of a sudden.'

'I think we can safely assume that the djinn had a hand in all that,' Taimur sneered.

Ness didn't know what to say. She had been told that her grandparents had died in a coaching accident. Something had run out in front of them, startling the horses. The coach had turned over, throwing the coachman clear but killing the passengers.

'But with only one wish, how would Bonehill have returned him to the bottle?' Hafid mused. 'Perhaps it was a pact of some kind, and I suspect that Lumm was involved somehow. That would explain why the djinn attacked him too.'

Ness knew that others were involved – she thought of the letter she had taken from Lumm's desk. It warned Mrs Olwen Quilfy that the djinn was coming for her. If she could find this lady, then the djinn would appear eventually. If it wasn't too late already. The vague inklings of a plan began to form in her mind.

'You appear lost in thought, young lady,' Hafid said, turning his ear to her. 'Do you know of anyone else who might be involved?'

The words of the djinn echoed in Ness's mind. Azuli may have rescued her at Lumm's house but these old, decrepit Lashkars couldn't stop the djinn. She had to do this on her own.

'Only Uncle Carlos ever came to the house,' Ness murmured, casting her eyes down. 'I just knew Lumm by name. I can't recall any other acquaintances. I was too young to notice.'

'We waste time with this cross-examining, Hafid,' Taimur cried, throwing his hands up. 'We need to find that damnable creature!'

'Patience, Taimur,' Hafid said, rubbing his temples and frowning. 'Believe me, I am trying to seek out the djinn by all means possible. I can sense him, but he is still weak. I reach out to him with my mind.'

'And what if your great mind can't find him?' Taimur grumbled. Ness could see spots of red beneath Taimur's grey beard. He trembled with frustration and rage.

'The djinn gave Miss Bonehill seven days,' Hafid whispered. 'If all else fails, he will come for her when the time is up – and we will be ready.'

'But what about my parents?' Ness gasped. 'I won't just sit here and wait while they're at that creature's mercy!'

'We will confront the djinn before then, Miss Bonehill,' Jabalah said, clasping his hands together. 'I am sure of it!'

'But you must stay with us in the meantime,' Hafid said, his voice low.

'Azuli,' Taimur whispered, 'bring the silver sword.'

Azuli bowed and scurried into a side room, leaving Ness sitting in awkward silence as Taimur paced back and forth.

'We cannot use the blade until we have found the djinn,' Hafid said, shaking his head.

'I just feel better with it in my grasp,' Taimur replied. Ness could see that he had once been a great warrior but now his wrists were stick thin within the baggy cuffs of his shirt.

Azuli returned with the sword cradled in both his arms, a richly decorated cloth swaddling the blade. Taimur eased the cloth back. Ness could see a dull, tarnished blade swirled with intricate carvings. With a sigh, Taimur lifted the blade from Azuli's outstretched arms and slashed the air. Ness recognised the curved scimitar shape from her lessons with Major Morris.

'Careful, Taimur,' Jabalah said, ducking theatrically. 'You'll take someone's head off.'

'I'd forgotten how heavy it is,' Taimur panted.

Ness frowned, remembering Major Morris telling her how light a sword the scimitar was.

Taimur swung the blade again, carving a clumsy figure of eight above his head. With a curse, he lost his balance, stumbling towards Ness, who threw herself to one side. The blade whistled past her ear. Taimur landed with a loud thump and the clatter of the silver sword rang around the room.

'Father!' Azuli cried, leaping forward.

Taimur shook him off as he scrambled to his feet, embarrassment reddening his face. 'I'm fine!' he snapped, stooping to pick up the sword.

'Let me carry the sword, Father,' Azuli said, extending his hand.

Taimur pulled away from him, his breath ragged, his eyes wide. 'You think I'm too old and infirm, is that it?' he growled.

'No, I just –'

'He didn't mean anything by it, Taimur,' Jabalah cut in.

'I swung that blade before you were born,' Taimur raged, flecks of spit flying from his lips. 'When our children stood at our sides.'

'But that was a long time ago!' Azuli pleaded, paling. 'Father –'

'Before we found you, abandoned at the dockyard,' Taimur yelled. 'You think I'm no longer strong enough to carry the last sword of Sulayman but I am a true Lashkar.'

'Taimur, enough!' Hafid croaked, raising his hand.

Jabalah jumped to his feet but the anger had fled from Taimur.

Taimur slapped the flat of the blade against Azuli's chest. 'Polish it,' he hissed. 'I want that djinn to see his own terrified reflection in that blade before I hack the head from his plague-ridden body.'

Azuli gripped the sword, his face taut. For a moment, Ness thought he was going to say something but he turned on his heel and stamped out of the room, slamming the door behind him.

Ness paused in the stunned silence that filled the room, then she hurried after Azuli. She had one chance and she was going to take it now.

A WOLF HUNGERS AFTER THE LAMB EVEN WITH HIS LAST BREATH.

TRADITIONAL PROVERB

CHAPTER FOURTEEN
THE BLOODY VICAR

Ness found Azuli sulking by two huge barrels at the side of the courtyard. The sword lay on top of the barrels and he smoothed the cloth over the carved metal. Ness couldn't read the script along the blade.

'What does it say?' she muttered, standing awkwardly next to the sullen boy. His thick mop of black hair and scowling expression made him look like a sulky eight-year-old.

'*It is not wise to name the djinn until you are about to strike*,' he mumbled, sliding the fabric down the blade. 'Not that I will ever get to use it.'

'I think they are wrong to overlook you,' Ness said.

Azuli stopped polishing. 'Really?' He sighed and dropped the cloth on to the barrel. 'They are so weak now,' he said. 'These last few years have taken their toll on the Lashkars. Harsh winters, the damp and stink from that foul river. You saw my father just now. He could barely hold this thing above his shoulder. How is he to fight a djinn?'

'But he can't see beyond his own pride,' Ness agreed. 'None of them can. Not even Hafid and he's meant to be wise!'

Azuli's face darkened. 'He is wise,' he muttered, then sighed again. 'I feel so disloyal. I wish I could just take the sword and hunt the djinn myself!'

'And why don't you?' Ness asked, raising her eyebrows at him.

Azuli's eyes lit up. 'Take the sword?' he said, lifting the blade so that the morning light glinted on it, dazzling Ness. 'If I knew where the djinn was then –'

'I found a name at Lumm's house,' Ness interrupted, excited at how easily Azuli accepted the idea. 'Probably the next victim. We could go together, lie in wait for the djinn . . .'

'And kill him!' Azuli hissed, his eyes aglow.

'No, I need to know where my parents are first,' Ness said. 'If you kill him, how will I ever know that?'

'Then what do you suggest?' Azuli sneered.

'Surely the djinn will fear the sword?' Ness reasoned. 'He may make some kind of deal, perhaps agree to be bound or return to his bottle rather than die.'

'I'm not sure,' Azuli snorted, wrapping the sword and thrusting it into his belt. 'But we must certainly leave before we are missed.'

'That may be easier said than done,' Ness said, grabbing Azuli's arm. 'How do we get out through the main gate?'

'We don't.' Azuli winked at her. 'I know another way out.'

He led her through the silent alleys, their footsteps echoing as they went, until they came to a dead end. Barrels and old packing cases cluttered the passage.

'This is a joke, I suppose?' Ness grumbled. 'How can we get out here? Do we climb over that wall?'

Azuli grinned and dragged a large barrel from against the wall to reveal a small square doorway about waist height to Ness.

'I used to sneak through here as a small boy,' he said, crouching down and pushing the rotten wooden door open.

'Not very dignified,' Ness muttered, bundling up her skirts and scurrying through after Azuli. If only she could wear her trousers, she'd be able to move about more freely.

She straightened up and dusted herself down. They stood in a similarly cut-off alley but the difference stunned her. This side of the wall stank of discarded rubbish and worse. The walls were black with slime and soot.

'We keep our own homes clean.' Azuli grinned. 'It is healthier. Why your people cannot do the same is beyond me.'

'Me too, but they aren't my people,' Ness replied. The whole place disgusted her. She was beginning to long for the wide-open skies and fresh air of the marshlands around Rookery Heights.

'Where are we going then?' Azuli said.

Ness pulled out the letter she had found at Lumm's. 'To see a Mrs Olwen Quilfy,' she said. 'And let's just pray that the djinn hasn't got to her first.'

Badenock Terrace was a row of prim houses that faced on to a neatly trimmed square. Anonymous and tucked away, it had taken them the best part of the day to find this innocuous line of red brick. Warmth glowed from every window and Ness found herself envying the families gathered together inside. In the darkening evening, the terrace looked commonplace but comforting somehow. Smart ponies pulled polished traps around the square and the few people walking the streets tipped their hats to each other.

'This hardly seems like the home of someone who has dealings with a djinn,' Ness said, wrinkling her nose.

'The unrighteous take many forms,' Azuli murmured, narrowing his eyes at the cheerful lamplight of Number Four. 'And none can be trusted. We shall ask our questions and then move on.'

'And who are the unrighteous?' Ness arched her eyebrows at Azuli.

'Any who deal with the djinn for personal gain,' he said, not meeting her steady gaze.

'Me, for example, or my father?'

'Your father, yes.' Azuli looked up, his eyes blazing. 'Not you, I suppose. You didn't open the bottle with full knowledge of what might happen. But we still don't know what it was you wished for.'

A woman's scream from Number Four cut Ness's response dead.

The two of them ran up to the front door. Faces appeared at the other windows of the terrace and one or two passers-by stopped, glancing around. Azuli banged on the front door as Ness stared in through the ground-floor window.

A clergyman rocked on his heels in a smart living room, his shocked face and white collar spattered with blood. He looked wide-eyed and disbelieving at something on the floor. He glanced up and Ness caught a glint of recognition as their eyes met. Then the man dashed from view.

'The back of the house,' Ness yelled. 'Quickly.'

'What?' Azuli snapped.

'No time to explain! Just follow me,' she cried.

Ness jumped down the steps and, clutching her skirts, sprinted the length of the terrace to an alleyway that snaked off behind the houses. She could hear Azuli's heavy tread close behind her.

They rounded the back of the terrace and almost ran into the blood-splattered vicar. Azuli drew the scimitar and crouched, pointing the wicked blade at the man.

'Whose blood is that, I wonder?' Azuli growled.

'I'll wager it belongs to Mrs Olwen Quilfy, late of this parish,' Ness hissed. 'Recently demised, you might say.'

The clergyman raised his hands, the red spots of blood contrasting with his thin, white face. 'It wasn't me, you have to believe me,' he gabbled. 'It was a demon, a thing not of this world. I'm a man of the cloth for goodness' sake!'

Ness narrowed her eyes. 'What happened?' she snapped.

A police whistle sounded some distance away.

The vicar's eyes widened. 'Can we get away from here?' he pleaded, his features crumpling with despair. 'I don't think the local constabulary will believe my tale any more than you will when I tell it, but *you* are unlikely to hang me.'

'That is no concern of ours,' Azuli said, scowling.

'It will be if they catch you too,' the vicar said, panic rising in his voice. 'They might just believe that a minister of the church – and a gentleman – is incapable of murder but what of a Lashkar boy wielding such a fine blade?'

The whistle sounded again. Ness glanced over to Azuli, who looked back, his face a picture of indecision.

'Very well,' she said. 'Let's go.'

'Thank the Lord,' the vicar gasped and hurried past them back on to the street, mopping his face with a handkerchief as he went. 'My carriage is waiting for me just around the corner.'

'You weren't planning on staying long then?' Ness called as they hurried after him.

'Think what you like,' he said over his shoulder. 'But I didn't kill Mrs Quilfy.' He nodded to the carriage driver and clambered in. Ness jumped in after him, followed by Azuli.

Heavy footsteps rang on the cobbles as the driver slammed the door shut and Ness caught a glimpse of blue uniforms and ruddy complexions flying past them towards

Mrs Quilfy's house. The clergyman slumped back in his seat and heaved a sigh of relief as the carriage lurched into motion.

'Who are you and what happened to Mrs Quilfy?' Azuli demanded, the scimitar still glinting free from its sheath.

'My name is Cullwirthy,' the vicar said, sweeping his lank, brown hair from his eyes and adjusting his spectacles. 'The Reverend Cullwirthy. I minister – ministered – to Mrs Quilfy.' He lowered his head and put his hands to his face.

'So what happened, Reverend?' Ness said. This man didn't seem to pose so much of a threat now.

'Mrs Quilfy was a troubled soul,' he murmured, looking away from them. 'The story of what happened to her is hard to believe. And it's a horrible story.'

Save your tears for your pillow and let the dead slumber on.

Traditional proverb

CHAPTER FIFTEEN

OLWEN QUILFY AND SWEET WILLIAM

'Olwen wasn't always so well-to-do. Her husband, William, died when he was quite young and they only enjoyed a few years of wedded bliss,' Cullwirthy said. 'The loss of her dear, sweet William tormented her and led her to investigate the darker pathways – the occult, witchcraft.'

'So you killed her?' Azuli hissed, raising his blade.

'This was many years ago,' Cullwirthy said, a spasm of irritation crossing his mild features, 'before you were born. She fell in with a gentleman called Anthony Bonehill, a gentleman in the loosest sense of the term. He came from a wealthy family but he was a ne'er-do-well.'

'How do you know that?' Ness snapped. She could feel her face colouring.

'The name means something to you,' Cullwirthy murmured, raising an eyebrow. 'Bonehill had a bottle – so Olwen told me – a bottle containing a djinn.'

Cullwirthy stopped and scanned Ness's face. 'You don't seem surprised.'

'We know something of this djinn you talk about,' Azuli said, keeping his face expressionless.

'I thought as much, else why would you be at Olwen's door at that very moment? Olwen told me that Bonehill's research revealed that the djinn would grant one wish to whoever opened the bottle and then he would kill them,' Cullwirthy continued. 'But Bonehill had a plan. He chose seven people –'

'Seven people would open the bottle,' finished Ness.

'Very clever, miss,' Cullwirthy muttered, eyeing Ness. 'Your mind works along similar lines as Mr Bonehill's. I'm sorry, I didn't catch your name in all the confusion . . .'

'Never mind that,' snapped Ness.

'So seven people open the bottle,' Azuli snarled. 'Seven people die. So what?'

'Not if the last of the seven wishes the djinn back in the bottle,' Ness whispered, staring at Cullwirthy.

'What's in it for the last man?' Azuli said. Ness could tell he was cross that he hadn't worked out the plan.

'Nothing.' Ness frowned. 'Not unless the others rewarded him.'

'What did Mrs Quilfy wish for?' Azuli said.

Cullwirthy's pale, waxy skin seemed to turn a more deathly colour as he spoke. 'Not great wealth or health. She wanted her dear William back.'

'And?' Ness dreaded the answer.

'Djinns are devious,' Azuli whispered. 'They will grant your wish but not always how you expect.'

'It's a tale as old as tales themselves,' Cullwirthy said, his voice low. 'William returned one night after years mouldering in his grave, decayed and screaming in agony. A monster driven insane by his newly given life and the putrefied state of his body.'

'That's terrible,' Ness gasped.

'Those who dabble with dark forces find themselves and those they love ensnared in a web,' Azuli said. 'A web that becomes more tangled and complex the more you try to unravel it.'

'Olwen kept William in her cellar for many months, not knowing what to do, who to turn to,' Cullwirthy continued. 'He was a hideous, living corpse who begged to be released back to the afterlife.'

'But surely my f— Mr Bonehill could have helped her,' Ness said, colouring at the slip of her tongue.

Cullwirthy gave a humourless laugh. 'Bonehill? Help? That man doesn't have a charitable bone in his body. He told her it was a foolish wish that she should have considered more carefully and that he wanted nothing more to do with her.'

'So what happened?' Ness felt faint.

'I took care of Olwen,' Cullwirthy said, his face hardening. 'I bought the house she lived in and made sure she had an income but the creature in the cellar wouldn't just go away. One night, I took a pistol down there and put a bullet through its brain.'

'You killed William?' Azuli said.

'He was dead already. I simply released him. It was a mercy that should have been performed months before,' Cullwirthy said through gritted teeth. 'But she never spoke to me again. After all I'd done for her. I loved her. But she wouldn't even see me. Not until today.'

Ness glanced around the plush carriage. 'You seem very comfortably off for a clergyman, Reverend Cullwirthy,' she muttered. 'This carriage is fit for a lord and you paid for Mrs Quilfy's house.'

'I made a sensible wish,' Cullwirthy said, slipping a pistol from his pocket. The carriage had stopped. 'Now get out. We'll continue this conversation in the house.'

Cullwirthy's vicarage stood shoulder to shoulder with similar imposing town houses, looming tall over the busy street. The Reverend draped his jacket over his arm, concealing the pistol as he stepped out into the street.

'You distract him,' Azuli whispered. 'I'll take his hand off at the wrist before he knows what's happening.'

'No,' Ness hissed back, grateful that Morris had given her some training in small arms. 'That's a Smith and Wesson revolver. If you miss, he'll have more than one bullet to waste on us.'

'Just keep moving,' Cullwirthy murmured. 'And don't try any clever sword work.'

They walked reluctantly up the steps to the front door and Cullwirthy turned a key in the lock.

'I let my staff go home at night,' he said, noticing Ness's searching glances around the dark-panelled hallway. 'My driver will have stabled the horses and gone by now. We're quite alone. Place that sword in the umbrella rack, boy, and we'll go into the drawing room.'

A cheerful fire cracked and spat in the hearth of the drawing room. Tables and chairs cluttered together busily as if a party had just finished. If it weren't for the fact that she had a gun pointed at her, Ness would have been quite comfortable there.

'So you were one of the Seven, Reverend?' Ness said.

'Yes, Miss Bonehill.' Cullwirthy smiled. 'I'm right, aren't I? You are his daughter. You resemble your mother more although you're somewhat darker. I never believed that silly tale about your death. It's quite beyond me why they concocted it.'

'To protect me from the likes of you, no doubt,' Ness said icily.

Cullwirthy nodded as if rolling the idea around in his head. 'He certainly had enough enemies who would do anything to hurt him but I never credited Anthony Bonehill with any paternal instincts. *Necessity*.' Cullwirthy spat her name out. It stung Ness like an insult.

'But what do you want with us now?' Azuli said, glaring at Cullwirthy. 'And why did you pretend not to know about the djinn when you were one of the Seven?'

'I hardly imagine you would have followed me to my home had I said, "Oh yes, I killed Mrs Quilfy. Now could you just pop along with me – I have an idea."' Cullwirthy sneered, smoothing his hair back over his forehead.

'You did kill her then?' Ness gasped, dismayed she had not trusted her instincts.

'The djinn is coming.' Cullwirthy's voice cracked a little. 'Your parents have vanished and I heard about Henry Lumm – horrible, simply awful. I wanted to save Olwen from such a fate. I wanted her to join me and find a way to stop the djinn. I told her I loved her. But she spat in my face, called me a murderer – me!'

'So you killed her,' Ness said, frowning.

'Better that than the djinn getting to her.' Cullwirthy licked his lips. The gun trembled in his hand. 'I lost my patience. I grabbed the poker by the fire and hit . . . But then I saw you . . . the Bonehill family resemblance was unmistakable. And the Lashkar boy with a silver scimitar. I couldn't believe my luck!'

'What do you mean?' Ness edged towards the door.

'Keep still,' Cullwirthy said, jabbing the barrel of the gun towards her. 'The djinn will be more than interested in the two of you. Maybe I can catch his attention enough to strike a deal and, if not, then the silver sword with his name on it should be enough to slay him. Oh, don't look so surprised, Lashkar boy. Bonehill told us all about your lot and their antics.'

The lamp grew faint and a chill fell over the room. The fire sputtered and began to smoke as if cold water had been poured over it. The smoke boiled and grew, filling the room, making Ness and Azuli cough.

Cullwirthy cackled, pointing at the shape that solidified in the fog before their eyes. 'Talk of the devil and he's sure to appear.'

Malice drinks its own poison.

Traditional proverb

CHAPTER SIXTEEN
DEATH DEALS

The smoke swirled and twisted as the figure grew more substantial. Ness saw the same features of the doll-like creature in her dream but he had filled out and grown in height. Stitches still bound his eyelids together. A grin full of needle teeth spread across his skeletal face. A ragged loincloth was all he wore and boils punctuated the yellowing skin that stretched across his bony frame.

'The Reverend Cullwirthy,' the djinn hissed. 'You look well. Has your life been all you hoped?'

'I have no complaints,' Cullwirthy said, sweat coursing down his brow.

'I've just visited the Quilfy household,' the djinn said, his reedy voice mocking Cullwirthy. 'But there was no one at home. I was quite put out.'

'She's beyond your cruelty now, you demon,' Cullwirthy spat.

The djinn inclined his head as if in agreement. 'True, but then she hardly had much of a life with her beloved William. Still, you have problems of your own now.'

'Perhaps,' Cullwirthy said. 'But then I thought we might cut a deal, you and I.' The pistol shook in his grasp but he had pointed it away from Ness. From the corner of her eye, she noticed Azuli edging towards the door.

'A deal?' The djinn's grin almost split his scabbed face and his topknot of hair shook as he laughed. 'What have you got that I would possibly be interested in?'

Azuli had moved out of Ness's vision now. Her heart hammered at her ribs. If he could make it to the hall and the sword, they might have a chance.

'The girl, for one,' Cullwirthy said, nodding in Ness's direction.

'Ah, Necessity Bonehill,' the djinn said, bowing low and chuckling to himself. 'We've already met, Cullwirthy. You're too late on that score. She has four more days by my reckoning. Have you found your parents yet, Necessity?' He laughed and turned back to Cullwirthy. 'You have nothing to bargain with and my power is growing. Behold.' The djinn waved his long fingers at the vicar, who gave a whimper and held up a hand as if to ward off the djinn's attack.

Ness stared in horror as Cullwirthy's hand stiffened and then turned black. The skin took on a polished hue then, with a sickening crack and squelch, the fingers merged into two long claws. Bristly hairs sprang from the skin. Cullwirthy's jacket sleeve shrivelled into his arm as it became stick thin, black and shining. More bristles sprouted. With a crack, his left leg gave beneath him. Cullwirthy howled in agony as his body cracked and twisted, forcing him to the floor.

'No, please,' Cullwirthy shrieked. 'I have something. I do!'

Ness gave a scream as a new leg burst from Cullwirthy's other side.

'Look at you now,' the djinn spat. 'Out of all of them I despised you almost as much as Bonehill. A hypocrite, sermonising every Sunday while enjoying the spoils of your evil ways and lusting after Widow Quilfy. What could a worthless insect like you possibly offer me?'

Ness felt sick. Cullwirthy's head now poked out of the fat, bloated body of a beetle. Fronds and bristles waved from the shining black thorax.

Cullwirthy's voice had taken on a croaking tone. 'A Lashkar boy . . . with a silver sword.'

'WHAT?' The djinn reared up, seeming to grow in stature.

Ness threw herself behind an armchair as Azuli burst back into the room, howling and swinging the sword – or was it the scimitar that howled?

For a moment, Ness saw real terror on the djinn's face. He launched himself backward as the sword cut through the smoky air.

'I know you, djinn, and your name is Zaakiel.' Azuli's voice sounded strong and full of authority. 'Allah can see you and you shall perish.'

Another swing narrowly missed the djinn, sending him tumbling over tables and chairs. Hurling a plant pot at Azuli, the djinn pointed at Cullwirthy, who writhed and quivered on the floor. With an ever-diminishing scream, the Reverend began to shrink. Ness screwed her eyes shut as the djinn slammed his foot down hard on the place where Cullwirthy had been and the screaming stopped.

'So the Lashkars of Sulayman still march?' the djinn snarled. His laughter had gone now.

'You are the last djinn. This is the last sword,' Azuli said, carving an arc just inches from the djinn's head.

'The last sword, eh? But you're a mere boy,' the djinn scoffed. 'Are the Lashkars so desperate? Will they send old women to stop me next?'

'Azuli, don't listen!' Ness cried. She could see the danger. Zaakiel was goading him. Anger and precise swordsmanship never mixed; Ness had learned that very early in her training.

'The Lashkars will vanquish you, Zaakiel!' Azuli yelled, his face reddening.

He swung the sword sideways and Zaakiel raised his wrist to meet the blow. Azuli gave a cry of victory as the djinn's hand went spinning off across the room, spattering green blood over carpet, walls and furniture. The djinn doubled over with a scream of agony. For a moment he remained still and Ness held her breath. *Is he dying?* But then the creature began to shake. *No, he's laughing*, Ness thought. Slowly the djinn raised his head, grinning.

'Your mistake,' he panted, clamping his remaining hand

over the stump of his wrist. Azuli stood staring helplessly as the blade in his hand began to vanish. 'The blade is melting but it hasn't slain me. Now I have something for you.' He stretched forward and opened his mouth, spitting a fountain of foul-smelling green slime at Azuli.

The boy fell back as boils bubbled up on his face and arms, sweat soaking his clothes. He dropped the scimitar handle and gripped his throat.

'No!' Ness threw herself at the djinn but he exploded into smoke as soon as she made contact with him.

'I would flee if I were you, little Necessity,' Zaakiel chuckled. 'He will die and become one of mine. You think me evil and twisted, but life is hard and it will not leave you unscathed, believe me.'

'Release him, you monster!' Ness yelled as the djinn swirled around her.

'I never wished for this,' he hissed. 'My silent prayers went unheeded across the gulf of three thousand years. All because I wouldn't bow to a tyrant.'

'A tyrant?' Ness squatted down and cradled Azuli in her arms.

'Sulayman. A great magician. A wise man. A bully,' Zaakiel said. 'We worked with him at first, carving cities out of mountains, turning deserts into lush jungles, building an empire together. But Sulayman became powerful and proud. He wanted us to bow down to him. "I have the wisdom and blessing of Allah," he told us. "I command man, afrit, animal and tree. I am a mighty potentate." And then we were afraid. We fled in terror of our lives, killing any who would try to catch us and bring us to kiss Sulayman's feet. But caught we were. For their disobedience my friends and family were sealed in the tiniest of vessels for all time. Trapped by Sulayman's curse.'

'I won't let him die,' Ness snapped, scooping Azuli up in her arms. 'Whatever happened thousands of years ago, it doesn't give you the right to do what you just did. It's wrong.'

'You will understand soon, Necessity Bonehill.' The djinn began to fade. 'Believe me, you will. The time of mankind is coming to an end.'

Ness staggered to the front of the vicarage, Azuli in her arms. She could feel the clamminess of his skin, the rattling of his breath. He was dying.

PRIDE WENT OUT ON HORSEBACK AND RETURNED ON FOOT.

TRADITIONAL PROVERB

CHAPTER SEVENTEEN
FEVER

Struggling with the weight of Azuli's limp body, Ness staggered into people, barging crowds of angry gentlemen aside as she tried to keep hold of him. His breath groaned from his body and she feared that each would be his last. He felt hot then cold and sometimes he would squirm and cry out in his delirium. The gaslights blazed as she pushed through a sea of shocked faces, focusing on her aching arms and legs so as to avoid remembering the images of Cullwirthy's hideous death.

On she stumbled, gasping, until at last the buildings became more familiar. Once more she found herself in the winding maze of alleys and uttered a silent prayer that she didn't meet Harmy Sullivan and his gang tonight.

Azuli stared up at her blankly and threw an arm out, making her drop him.

'Don't die, you stubborn fool,' Ness panted as she

dragged him by the shoulders through the muddy alleyways. 'I'll never forgive you if you go now.'

The alcove and the barrels finally came into view and Ness threw herself at the blue gate.

Jabalah's face appeared before her. 'Miss Bonehill, where have you been?' He stopped when he saw Azuli lying at her feet. Without further questions, he grabbed Azuli and ran through the streets, leaving Ness to trail after.

The night kept people in their homes but it didn't stop them from peering through windows as Ness passed. More bad news had spread, it seemed. Ness saw Jabalah disappear into Hafid's house with his feverish burden and she followed.

'What have you done?' Taimur screamed as Ness entered the room. Two Lashkars held his arms, otherwise she thought she might have had to defend herself. Azuli lay murmuring on a sofa, shaking his head from side to side.

Ness slumped on to a chair without being asked to sit down and buried her head in her hands. 'I didn't force him to come,' she sighed. 'We found the djinn. Azuli fought bravely.'

'And the fiend?' Hafid asked, hope edging his voice as he stood at Azuli's head, knitting his fingers together.

'He tricked Azuli.' Ness groaned. 'He was wounded but not killed.'

'The djinn lives,' Hafid hissed. 'And now the sword is gone.'

'My son,' Taimur cried, falling to Azuli's side and hugging him close. 'So young.'

'He was brave.' Hafid laid a hand on Taimur's shoulder.

'There must be something we can do!' Ness cried.

'There is no cure for the djinn's plague,' Hafid said, shaking his head. 'It is only my protective charms that stop him spreading among us here.'

'Spreading?' Ness echoed.

'The plague is highly contagious, Miss Bonehill,' Hafid whispered. 'How many people did you brush against and bump into on your way here?'

'Oh my Lord. No,' Ness gasped. 'That's what the djinn meant. He wanted me to take Azuli away. The time of man is coming to an end.'

'You carried Azuli and the contagion through the city,' Hafid said, his voice half resigned, half angry. 'Soon it will spread, killing man, woman and child, rich and poor, heathen and believer, creating an army of Pestilent walkers to do the djinn's bidding.'

'I didn't know . . . I didn't mean to –' Ness began.

'Just like you didn't mean to open the bottle and let the djinn out,' Taimur spat.

'I wish I hadn't,' Ness said, tears stinging her eyes. 'I really do.'

'Wishes,' Hafid muttered, staring at Ness with his blind eyes. 'That's where this all began. A web of wishes that has entangled so many people. We all have wishes, Necessity Bonehill. I wish Azuli was fit and well again, I wish we could find another way to destroy the djinn.

I wish we could win in the end. But wishes rarely come true in the way we want them to.'

Ness hung her head. The room seemed to spin and she screwed her eyes shut, only to see the djinn's leering grin; Cullwirthy twisting and writhing as he transformed; Azuli's grey face, bathed in sweat and blistered with sores. Faster and faster the images whirled and spun around in her mind's eye until she felt like she was falling, tumbling into a dark abyss. The last thing she saw was Jabalah leaping forward, his arms outstretched to catch her as she fainted.

Ness floated in a dream through mist and fog. Once more she felt cold and alone, unable to see a hand right in front of her. The djinn's voice whined in her ear like a mosquito, sometimes far off, sometimes close to.

'In the darkness of my first century trapped in the bottle, I vowed that anyone who let me out would have a thousand of my blessings and three wishes.

'And sure enough, after two hundred years of waiting, of listening to the tide rush against the walls of my tiny prison, I felt the pull of a net drag me to the surface of the dark sea.

'The light blinded me, burned my skin, sent me screaming into the sky, but the joy of freedom made me immune to pain.

'A simple fisherman stood holding the bottle and staring at me, slack-jawed and drooling. His face creased into a mask of greed as I told him my tale of woe and gratitude.

'"My first wish?" He leered at me and then glanced down the coast. "My neighbour lives but a mile from here. He has

everything I have not. A beautiful wife, a fine boat, happy children. How I hate him. Bring me his head."

'"His head?" I repeated.

'"Has all that time in a bottle made you deaf?" the fisherman snapped.

'"Has this man wronged you?" I asked. "Has he taken something that is yours?"

'"You swore to grant me three wishes," the man said, narrowing his eyes at me. "Now do as I say."

'I still can't think of that first poor soul without a shiver of remorse. He sat quietly at his hearth after a hard day mending nets and pitching his boat. His pretty young wife sat teasing the children at his feet.

'Until I burst in, that is.

'"Now bring the wife and make her agree to marry me," the fisherman snarled when I returned with his neighbour's head. "Terrify her. Threaten to eat her children if she does not agree."

'Just you wait, I thought, as I returned to the house where the woman still crouched in the corner of the room, her wide-eyed children clinging to her.

'"You have done well." The fisherman grinned a crooked grin and hugged the woman to him. "Now return to your bottle."

'"What?" I couldn't believe what I was hearing. "But your third wish. You could have wealth and power, all that you desire."

'"I have this woman, her husband's boat and twice as much sea to fish now, thanks to you," laughed the fisherman. "And I can

sell you on to the next man who wants three wishes for a fortune and then that's his lookout. Now go, return to your bottle."

'With a heavy heart, I slipped back into my black prison and listened. I listened as he drove the poor woman to an early grave and her children became his slaves, all thanks to me.

'Time hardens you, Necessity Bonehill. Man's cruelty toughens your heart, burns it to a hard, blackened cinder.'

'Let Azuli live,' Ness cried, lashing her hands out into the white mist as if she could grab the djinn. 'I beg you. Let him live. You don't have to be so wicked.'

'*I don't think I can help myself any more,*' the djinn whispered. '*Besides, it seems the matter of Azuli is out of my hands. Four days to go, I believe.*'

Ness sat up suddenly, gasping for breath. Once more she lay in Jabalah's house. It was quiet. The morning's activity had begun outside. *Day four*, Ness thought. *What now? How can I ever get an answer to my question if I can't find my parents?*

She leapt up, calling for Suha.

Suha came running in from the kitchen, drying her hands. 'Necessity, what is it?'

'Azuli,' Ness gasped, grabbing Suha's shoulder. 'Where is he? I must see him.'

'Steady, my dear.' Suha smiled, trying to ease Ness back into her bed. 'It is a miracle but Azuli has come through the fever –'

Suha didn't get a chance to finish her sentence as Ness jumped up and hurried out into the street, ignoring the stares and the coldness of the cobbles on her bare feet. She barged past wide-eyed old men carrying bundles on their shoulders and women with crates of squawking chickens, straight to Hafid's quarters, past Jabalah, who stood open-mouthed as she thundered into Hafid's chamber.

Azuli was sitting up, devouring a huge chunk of fruit cake. Taimur sat grinning at his son. Ness threw herself forward and pulled Azuli into a tight hug, sending cake and plate spinning on to the floor.

'Azuli! Thank God you're all right. I thought you'd be . . .' Her voice trailed off as she became aware of the stony looks that greeted her.

'Miss Bonehill,' Jabalah said, wrapping a large blanket around Ness's shoulders. 'However pleased you might be to see Azuli fit and well, I'm not sure it is becoming to charge through the streets in your nightdress and to appear so unclothed before the Elders of the Lashkar.'

'Oh, sorry.' Ness gave a shy grin and glanced around, noticing Hafid was there. She pulled the blanket tight about her. 'But what happened? How did he recover?'

Azuli gave a beaming smile of his own. 'I'm tough. Allah must have given me the constitution of an ox. No djinn can defeat me.'

'The brains of an ox, I'd agree, running off with our greatest weapon,' Hafid murmured. 'Praise Allah that you survived but I suspect it was more than your robust good health that saved you, Azuli.'

'The djinn is toying with us perhaps,' Taimur said, getting to his feet. 'Like a cat with a mouse.'

'With the sword gone, we cannot defend ourselves,' Jabalah sighed, rubbing a fleshy palm across his forehead. 'Even with it, it was doubtful we could defeat the djinn.'

'Our options are greatly reduced but there is still some slight hope,' Hafid said. 'We must continue to seek the djinn and fulfil our promise. We must try to destroy him or we must die in the attempt.'

ARROGANCE DIMINISHES WISDOM.

TRADITIONAL PROVERB

CHAPTER EIGHTEEN

ENEMY AT THE GATE

'Hope?' Taimur glowered at Hafid. 'What hope is there? Without the sword, what weapons do we have against the djinn?'

'The wisdom of Sulayman is ancient,' Hafid croaked, stroking his chin. 'But we have forgotten much of it over the centuries. We have relied too much on one weapon. Our people have hunted and fought many djinns. They can't all have found victory with one clean blow of a silver sword!'

'There are other ways to stop the djinn?' Ness said, a shiver of excitement running down her spine.

'There is always another way,' Hafid murmured, staring intently at Ness. She shivered, forgetting he was blind. 'Your father, for all his faults, knew that. Or how could he have outsmarted the djinn in the first place?'

'We think that Father asked seven people to open the bottle,' Ness said, not liking the way Hafid spoke about her father as if he were gone already. 'The last one would have wished it back into the bottle and the others were supposed to share their new good fortune with him.'

'Ingenious,' Hafid murmured, shaking his head. 'What is it about the number seven?'

'The djinn gave me seven days,' Ness said, her heart sinking. 'Did he need time to settle old scores? Did he put off granting my wish so he could kill Lumm and Cullwirthy? He would have got Quilfy too if the vicar hadn't done it first. If only I'd known.'

Hafid lifted his head, and if Ness hadn't known he was blind she would have sworn he was staring at her. 'And what was it you wished for, Necessity? You still haven't told us.'

'If I'd known what I do now, I'd have wished for the djinn's death,' Ness whispered, casting a backward glance to the gates and the horrors beyond. 'As it was, I made a foolish wish about my parents.'

Hafid nodded and smiled. 'You wished they loved you?'

Ness gave a start and felt her face flush red.

Hafid sighed. 'Not foolish at all, if I understand things correctly.'

'Thank you,' Ness muttered, staring at the ground.

'But time is not on our side. Bonehill was a clever man but he did not defeat the djinn alone,' Hafid said, raising his voice. 'We must make a trip to Jesmond Street.'

'Jesmond Street?' Ness said, frowning.

'A wise man lives there,' Hafid said, nodding his bald head. 'An antiquarian scholar and an old acquaintance of your father's. He may be able to help us.'

'Some dusty scholar of books and a friend of the Bonehill's into the bargain?' Taimur snorted. 'It's a warrior we need now, not some short-sighted old librarian!'

'Forgive me, Taimur,' Hafid said, giving a tight smile, 'but I fear it is you who is being short-sighted. It is brains, not brawn, that will win this battle.'

Ness opened her mouth to speak but an ashen-faced old man hobbled in and whispered to Jabalah, who turned a similar colour on hearing what he had to say.

'Hafid,' Jabalah said, his voice shaking. 'I have bad news. It seems we have company.'

'The djinn?' Hafid asked.

Jabalah shook his head. 'No, but it must be the work of the djinn. Come with me.'

Ness followed the old men as they shuffled out into the street. Jabalah led them to the blue gate, where a crowd jostled and stared through the peephole used by the guard. Cursing, Taimur pushed and shoved people out of their way until a path had been cleared. A green-tinged mist trickled under the gate, chilling them.

'It would seem the djinn has found us,' Hafid murmured, shaking his head.

Squeezing her way forward, Ness pressed her eye to the hole and gasped, nearly staggering back at the sight before her. The mist was thick outside but Ness could make out line upon ragged line of Pestilents, standing mute and still as stone. From the clothes, Ness could make out gentlemen, dockers, costermongers, servants and maids. They stood, milky-eyed, grey-skinned, their arms slack at their sides. Waiting.

'Zaakiel's army of the dead,' Azuli said, placing a steadying hand on Ness's shoulder.

'I'm told all three gateways are covered,' Jabalah murmured. 'Nobody can get in or out.'

'Why doesn't the djinn just come and face us?' Taimur snapped.

'The wound Azuli inflicted has weakened him,' Hafid said. 'Zaakiel must be containing us until he has recovered. Only then will he attack.'

'Then we are doomed.' Jabalah leaned heavily against the gate.

Taimur stepped forward and grabbed his shoulders. 'We will not give up so easily. Think of the sacrifices that have been made in the past. Think of our children. Hafid will keep the djinn out so we have some time to prepare,' he said. 'Do not give up hope, my friend.'

Azuli stepped to his father's side, staggering a little. 'I will fight with you, Father,' he said. 'I will make amends for the shame I have brought on you.'

Taimur smiled and ran his fingers through Azuli's black hair. 'You should never be ashamed of your bravery, my son. You have the heart and courage equal to any Lashkar.'

'We can all fight,' Ness said, her stomach tightening.

They couldn't win, she knew that. The number of Pestilents would grow as the contagion spread. The djinn would send an endless number to destroy them. When the time came, they would break down the gates and overrun Arabesque Alley. But she would rather fight than do nothing. The silence stifled her. Ness shivered, pulling the blanket tighter around her neck.

'This makes things more difficult,' Hafid said, resting on his stick. He suddenly looked so much older. 'At present, we are only safe if we stay within Arabesque Alley. Any who venture forth will no longer be under my protection and will succumb to the djinn's plague.'

'Not quite anyone,' Ness muttered, partly to herself.

Hafid lifted his head and gave a hopeful smile. 'You're right, Miss Bonehill,' he said. 'You have proved singularly resistant to the pestilence, as do most who command a wish. If we could get you out . . .'

'What?' Taimur stared at Hafid in disbelief. 'You aren't serious.'

'I survived the fever,' Azuli said, stepping forward. 'I don't believe it can harm me again.'

'Azuli, no!' Taimur cried.

'Please, Taimur,' Hafid said. 'They are both right. Nobody else is able to leave.'

'But the djinn will follow them,' Taimur said.

'The djinn is weak. This may be our only chance,' said Hafid. 'We will strengthen the gates and watch the Pestilents while Azuli and Miss Bonehill seek this man in Jesmond Street.'

'Please, Father.' Azuli grabbed Taimur's sleeve. 'I've learned my lesson. Caution will be my watchword. Let us go. Let me regain my honour.'

Taimur looked from Ness to Hafid to Azuli and heaved a long sigh. 'Very well,' he said at last. 'But if all looks lost, Hafid, I will not stand by and let those creatures overrun the alleys.'

'If all looks lost, Taimur, neither will I,' Hafid said.

'But how will you get Miss Bonehill and Azuli past the Pestilents?' Jabalah frowned.

'Azuli knows more than one way out,' Hafid said, giving a throaty chuckle.

'Indeed.' Azuli grinned and winked at Ness. 'But you'd better put on something other than a nightdress if we are going out into the city.'

The thick, foul-smelling fog filled Arabesque Alley and the surrounding streets when Ness, now dressed, met Azuli again. Women had gathered their belongings in sacks and baskets and were dragging them to the upper storeys of the buildings. Nobody screamed or shouted; they merely helped each other as quickly as they could. These people were used to danger, Ness knew. They packed up and moved on in the night, setting up home wherever they must. They had done it for centuries. But this time they were trapped.

At the gate, the old warriors watched the immobile mass just outside. Some sharpened their swords and cleaned their guns. Others struggled with beams of wood scavenged from their own homes and wedged them against the wood of the gate to guard against intruders.

Azuli stood gaping at Ness.

'What's wrong with you?' Ness snapped. 'Have you never seen a girl in trousers before?'

'I, erm, no,' Azuli stammered, his face reddening.

'Well, you'd better get used to it quickly. If we have to run or fight, I don't want to be struggling with long skirts again,' Ness said. 'I had enough trouble persuading Jabalah to donate a pair. He looked even more horrified when I cut the legs short.'

Jabalah hurried back from the gate through the mist, sweat beading his brow. 'It's still quiet,' he panted, revealing his age and lack of fitness. 'It is unnerving, the way they stand so still. You must hurry. Who knows how long the djinn will take to recover.'

'What are we asking this man for?' Azuli frowned.

'You have to be completely candid with him,' Jabalah said, placing a hand on Azuli's shoulder. 'Tell him everything. Hafid trusts this man. He may be able to think of some way to defeat the djinn.'

'And to rescue my parents,' Ness added.

Jabalah sighed and shook his head. 'Our priority has to be to stop the djinn.'

'But if we can force him to release them . . .' Ness said, narrowing her eyes.

'We'll find a way.' Azuli nodded.

Ness didn't miss the glance he gave Jabalah. *I'm not going to let you kill the djinn before I've found my parents*, she promised herself. Ness pulled a cap down low on her brow.

'Let's get going then,' she said, leading the way to the blocked alley with the small gateway.

Azuli pulled the barrels out of the way and Ness scrambled through. The alleyway on the other side of the wall lay empty except for a few rotting barrels leaking something putrid on to the slimy cobbles. Ness stooped to help Azuli up as he scrambled through after her.

'I bet all the djinn's attention is focused on the main gates,' he murmured. 'We'd better get a move on before he realises we're out.'

'I wouldn't be so sure,' Ness gasped, staring into the swirling fog. At first, all she could hear was the slip and scuff of boots on the cobblestones. Then a shadowy figure loomed out of the mist, moving towards them fast.

Azuli drew a sword. 'You try to get past,' he said, slashing at the air. 'I'll keep it occupied and try to catch up with you.'

'No,' Ness snapped. 'We go together or not at all.'

Azuli frowned, his eyes burning, but then he gave a grin. 'You are impossible,' he said, starting forward. 'You know that, don't you?'

'It has been mentioned.' Ness grinned, following him.

Her grin froze as a man charged out of the mist towards them. She glimpsed a shock of grey hair, a khaki uniform and a bristling moustache.

'Azuli, no! I think –' she cried, trying to grab him and pull him back.

But he slipped out of reach. With a yell, Azuli ran to meet the figure, flailing the air with his sword. The man stopped and swung his rifle up to parry the blow, then swung the butt into Azuli's stomach, sending him sprawling, helpless, to the ground.

A thousand regrets will not pay back a single debt.

Traditional proverb

CHAPTER NINETEEN
EVENYULE SCRABSNITCH

'I admire your spirit, sonny, but you need to be a bit more artful than that,' the man grunted, poking the rifle barrel to Azuli's nose.

'Major Morris!' Ness yelled, throwing herself at him. 'Thank goodness!'

'It's good to see you, my girl.' Morris dropped the rifle and wrapped her in his burly arms. 'They couldn't keep me locked up for long.'

'What happened? How did you get away?' Ness gabbled.

Morris's face grew grim as he shook his head. 'I managed to escape from those bumpkin constables but you'd taken my advice and jumped on a barge by then. I went to your house –'

'I know,' Ness cut in. 'The djinn burned it and he took my parents.'

'You think they're still alive?' Morris said, raising his eyebrows.

'I know it,' Ness said, remembering the words of the djinn in her dream.

'Thank God,' Morris muttered. 'I thought the Lashkars might have caught up with you, so I decided to track them down first. Took me a while, I'll confess. Well hidden, these blighters.'

'Excuse me,' Azuli groaned, scrambling to his feet and nursing his stomach. 'But who is this man? And what gives him the right to attack me?'

'Pardon me, sonny, but you charged at me swinging that sword,' Morris grunted, squinting at Azuli. 'You were lucky I didn't blow your bloomin' head off.'

Azuli glared at Morris. 'My name is Azuli,' he muttered, 'and I am not your son.'

'I know who you are, sonny,' Morris growled. 'An' I know all about your Lashkars. I fought alongside some of them in India.'

'If you know all about us, then you should treat me with more respect,' Azuli said, holding Morris's gaze. 'Besides, in this evil mist, how are you even still alive?'

'That's enough,' Ness snapped. 'We can talk on the way but we must get to Jesmond Street before the djinn recovers.'

'It's a fair question, Ness,' Morris said as they set off. 'Let's just say that my time with the Hinderton Rifles taught me a thing or two about warding off poisonous magical miasmas.'

The three figures drew some curious gazes as they strode along the London streets; a tall military man, dressed in khaki, with a bristling moustache and ruddy features, followed by a boy in a turban with a sword buckled to his belt and what looked like a ragged street urchin in cut-down trousers and a battered cap. As they went, Ness gave Morris a garbled account of all that had happened while also trying to explain to Azuli who this strange, imposing old man was.

The mist had confined itself to the immediate area of Arabesque Alley so that everything seemed normal on these streets. Housewives scurried among the street stalls, haggling with the fruit sellers; butchers' boys hurried through the crowd with legs of meat over their shoulders; people called and waved to each other. Ness felt a sudden pang of sadness. *How could anyone want to end all this life?*

'I've known your parents for many years, Ness,' Morris said as they weaved in and out of the crowd. 'I served under your father in India but it was your mother who showed me special kindness when I lost my daughter and grandchildren. I'll not reopen old wounds, if you don't mind.' Morris coughed roughly and Ness detected a twinkle of moisture in his eye. 'Suffice to say, she became like a second daughter to me and so when she asked me to watch out for you, I was more than happy to.'

'Mama asked you to teach me to fight and shoot?' Ness frowned, incredulous. 'Why would she do that?'

'She didn't ask me to.' Morris gave another cough. 'That was my idea. I could see what a free spirit you were. I knew I couldn't protect you for ever so I decided to give you the skills to defend yourself.'

'But you pretended to be mad?' Azuli said, trying to keep up with Morris and with the story.

'Was I pretending?' Morris said, raising an eyebrow. 'Mrs Bonehill was very particular that I didn't reveal that I was there to watch over Ness. It was a perfect cover.'

'But why?' Azuli shook his head.

'How do you think Ness would've reacted to the news that I was keeping an eye on her?'

Azuli grinned. 'She probably would have shot you with your own rifle.'

Morris grinned back at him. 'Something like that, I dare say. But your parents were also worried about Grossford finding you.'

'Uncle Carlos?' Ness said. 'But why wouldn't they want him to find me?'

'He sent you the bottle, didn't he?' Morris said. 'Carlos was a dangerous man by all accounts and often demanded money from your father, threatening him with the bottle and the djinn. I hate to say it, Ness, but the people your father mixed with weren't very pleasant and, well, neither was he.'

Ness bit her lip and then looked at her shoes. 'I know that, Sergeant Major,' she mumbled.

'Mrs Bonehill told you all about the djinn and you believed her?' Azuli said.

'I saw enough horror and mystery in the Hindertons to convince me that there's more to this world than meets the eye.' Morris's ruddy complexion paled. 'And I've learned to be careful what *I* wish for.'

'Well, it wouldn't do any harm to wish we were in more salubrious surroundings,' Ness said, wrinkling her nose as they turned into Jesmond Street. 'I fear this place has fallen on hard times.'

Jesmond Street had indeed seen better days. Costermongers bellowed their wares across the ragged crowd that seethed along its cobbles but the shops that lined the street sagged against each other. Roof tiles slipped to reveal the skeleton of beams beneath and paint peeled from window frames, the panes of glass grimed and opaque.

'But not, it seems, the emporium.' Ness frowned as she squeezed between two portly gents. 'Number Thirteen, there it is.'

The Emporium of Archaic Antiquities stood out on the row of crumbling shops like a lord visiting a workhouse. Its frontage gleamed, with artefacts lined up behind the shining window panes. It stood tall and proud as if turning its nose up at the desolation that surrounded it.

'It's a long time since I've been down this way.' Morris raised his eyebrows in surprise. 'Things have changed. It was always the emporium that struggled in the past.'

'You know it?' Ness stared at Morris, almost knocking a woman over in the crush.

'I brought a few . . . items back from my travels.' Morris looked rather shamefaced. 'Temple bowls and statues and such. The owner would buy them off me, polish them up and sell them on as something exotic and special.'

The bright ping of a brass bell heralded their arrival as they heaved open the door. The interior of the emporium was vast; it made Ness think of a cross between a church and a library. Bookshelves lined the walls, disappearing up into the shadows near the ceiling. Display cases stood in rows, full of curious objects and stuffed animals. Old chairs and suits of shining armour were dotted about the room. Light streamed in through the huge display windows at the front of the shop.

Across the room a fire crackled merrily and next to it, in a huge leather armchair, sat an ancient-looking man smoking a long-stemmed pipe. He wore a brightly coloured smoking jacket and a pillbox hat that balanced on top of a mass of wispy, white hair.

'Welcome to the Emporium of Archaic Antiquities,' the man said, his voice sonorous and dramatic. 'I am Evenyule Scrabsnitch, purveyor of the bizarre, the macabre and the downright inexplicable. How may I help you?'

'Is that you, Ted?' Morris said, squinting at the old man. 'Ted Oliver?'

'That *was* a name I used to go by,' he replied, and squinted back at Morris through a small pair of spectacles. His long face was exaggerated by a walrus moustache. 'Good Lord! It's Morris, isn't it? Charlie Morris.' He pulled himself to his feet and grabbed the sergeant's hand.

Morris shook it so vigorously that Ness worried the old man would fall over. 'I thought you'd be long gone.' Morris beamed, then his expression fell. 'Do pardon me, I didn't mean . . .'

Scrabsnitch laughed. 'No, no, I haven't gone yet.' He eyed Morris. 'I've had incredible good fortune.'

'Indeed.' Ness looked around her and chewed her lip.

'Forgive me.' Scrabsnitch struggled to his feet again and bowed to Ness and Azuli. 'Welcome to my emporium. Charlie calls me Ted Oliver but these days I'm known as Evenyule Scrabsnitch – something of an affectation I adopted in times gone by.'

'Before your incredible good fortune?' Ness murmured, raising one eyebrow at him.

'This is Necessity Bonehill and Azuli of the Lashkars of Sulayman,' Morris said.

Ness noticed Scrabsnitch flinch at the sound of her name and he spluttered on the smoke from his pipe.

'Charmed, I'm sure,' Scrabsnitch said, recovering himself and taking her hand. 'I knew your father.'

'I can tell,' Ness said, fixing him with her eye. 'And what was it *you* wished for, Mr Scrabsnitch?'

One ounce of good fortune is worth ten pounds of wisdom.

Traditional proverb

CHAPTER TWENTY

The Thing in the Cupboard

Scrabsnitch heaved a long sigh and seemed to sink further into his armchair.

'I'm not proud of what we did,' he said at last. '1854 was a bad year for me. Times were hard and so when my research with your father into the existence of the djinn came to fruition, I was only too happy to participate. Especially when your father came up with what seemed like a foolproof plan.'

'Plan?' Ness repeated.

'Yes. Our research had shown that the djinn gave a wish to whoever opened the bottle but that there were dangers. We read of an event in the 1830s in Spain in which a djinn slew the bottle holder after granting his wish.'

'My father still talks of that bottle,' Azuli murmured. 'It was a fearsome creature.'

'We didn't want to make the same mistake, so Anthony Bonehill hit upon the idea of more than one person opening the bottle at the same time. Everyone who opened it would have a wish and the last person would wish the djinn dead in an instant.'

'But the last person wouldn't get anything out of the deal,' Morris added, 'so he had to be sure that the others would make it worth his while.'

'So *that*'s how they did it!' Ness whispered. 'Uncle Carlos was the last one.'

'I pleaded with Bonehill to just keep it between the three of us,' Scrabsnitch sighed. 'His wife could have wished the djinn dead and all would have been well. But he had bragged to too many of his fellow researchers.'

'Did they all want a wish despite the danger?' Ness said, pulling a face.

'They weren't the most . . . selfless of people.' Scrabsnitch gave a cough.

'Anthony was scraping the barrel when he came to Grossford,' Morris murmured, tracing a finger along an old blunderbuss that hung on the wall.

'The Bonehills weren't blessed with a huge social circle,' Scrabsnitch said, avoiding Ness's eye. 'Some found Anthony abrasive in his manner, shall we say. Nevertheless he ended up with seven participants.'

'And Grossford wished the djinn back into the bottle rather than dead,' Morris concluded.

'He lost trust in the others,' Scrabsnitch said. 'I can't say that I blame him. The djinn drove a wedge between us. He insisted on seeing each of the Seven separately. He was devious. He twisted your words and confused you.

Anthony was going to make the last wish but when his wife came out of the cellar where the djinn was hiding, something wasn't right. Anthony was furious, screaming at her. Then he insisted on going in to wish before Grossford, and forced Grossford to make the last wish instead.'

'Grossford wouldn't have been happy with that,' Morris said, shaking his head.

'No, he wasn't,' Scrabsnitch sighed. 'But he was a coward. Anthony easily bullied him into it.'

'My father wanted to wish for something other than the death of the djinn,' Ness murmured. 'I wonder what it was Mama wished for that so upset him.'

'I don't know but I do remember being terrified that nobody would wish the djinn dead and it would all go wrong,' Scrabsnitch said with a sniff. 'I suspect your father wished for great wealth because, shortly afterwards, your mother inherited a huge fortune – in rather tragic circumstances, as I recall. At least Carlos got the djinn back in the bottle.'

'But he couldn't resist taking advantage,' Morris muttered, breathing on the barrel of the blunderbuss and giving it a polish with his cuff.

Scrabsnitch nodded. 'Carlos made everyone's life a misery, blackmailing them with the bottle. He would say that if anything happened to him he had made arrangements for it to be opened then. His demands became more and more excessive.'

'So somebody had him killed?' Ness said, folding her arms.

'It seems so,' Scrabsnitch mused. 'One of the Seven couldn't bear it any more.'

'You're the last of the Seven who is alive or free,' Azuli said, eyeing Scrabsnitch with suspicion. 'What did you wish for?'

'Incredible good fortune,' Scrabsnitch said, giving a little laugh and waving around the emporium. 'And it worked. I stumbled across amazing finds during my travels, frequently found money in the street. Even Grossford didn't bother me. I was always out when he came to call or some coincidence kept him away. Having Grossford killed would have been pointless.'

'But even your incredible good fortune won't keep the djinn away,' Ness said, frowning. 'In fact, it's incredibly lucky that you're still alive as it is, given that the others are all either missing or dead.'

'I suspected that the djinn was free again,' Scrabsnitch said, shaking his head. 'But what's the point of hiding? I've had a long life, good health and great wealth. He will come for me and that will be the end of it.'

'And you don't care that he'll be free to cause mayhem and chaos in the world?' Morris asked, pulling down the blunderbuss and peering into the trumpet-like barrel.

'The creature is spreading a devastating plague,' Ness said. 'All those infected by it become his slaves. Every day it claims more victims.'

'I am old,' Scrabsnitch sighed, shaking his head. 'What can I do?'

'We Lashkars wear our age like a badge of honour,' Azuli snorted. 'We would be ashamed to be so resigned to fate.'

'Hafid said you were wise, Mr Scrabsnitch,' Ness pleaded. 'He said you might have some answers. Please, is there anything that might aid us in defeating the djinn and saving my parents? You're our last hope!'

Scrabsnitch heaved another sigh, looking from Morris to Azuli and then to Ness. 'Necessity, you go to that large cupboard over there,' he said finally. 'The least we can do is look through some of the papers and books we amassed while researching this cursed djinn.'

Ness hurried around glass cabinets and bookcases to a huge cupboard. She stopped and frowned. Was it her imagination or did it shudder a little every now and then? It was only slight but she could sense a tremor as if something were inside, trying to get out.

'Is it safe?' she whispered, reaching a trembling finger towards the door of the cupboard.

'What?' Scrabsnitch squinted at her and then slapped a hand to his forehead. 'Of course, I'd forgotten. Don't worry, my dear, it's just a curiosity your father and I collected. It's been dormant for years.'

'Well, that doesn't reassure me,' Ness muttered but pulled the door open.

An avalanche of papers, documents and dust rained down on Ness, knocking her flat. But there was something writhing around in the midst of it all. Something black and tattered like some hideous giant grub bound with thick rope, twisting and wriggling. Ness scurried backward on all fours in her haste to get away.

'What is it?' she gasped.

'Step aside, Ness. I will deal with it,' Azuli said, drawing his sword.

'No!' Scrabsnitch yelled.

It was too late. Azuli's blade bit down on the strange black mass. The rope sprang into the air as if under great tension. It flicked back, whipping Azuli in the face and making him fall back with a cry. In an explosion of dust the thing seemed to unroll and flatten out into a rippling cloud of dust.

Gradually the years of dust dissipated into the air, leaving a ragged black carpet floating about their heads. It rippled and flapped in some mystical breeze that Ness couldn't feel. It looked torn and filthy, with no discernible pattern, just the coarse weave of ebony, rope-like material.

'Steady now,' Scrabsnitch whispered, crouching as if he were getting ready to dive for cover. 'Don't make any sudden moves.'

'What is it?' Ness hissed.

'A flying carpet?' Azuli said, his jaw slack.

'Look out!' Scrabsnitch yelled as the carpet launched itself towards Ness. Ness threw herself to the floor as it flashed past her, crashing through three display cabinets and disappearing up into the dark shadows of the high ceiling.

'Here it comes again!' Morris shouted, throwing himself under a table. The carpet came whistling back, knocking Scrabsnitch's hat from his head and sending the frail old man tumbling to the floor.

'It's deadly,' he croaked. 'Bonehill brought it back from the Hindu Kush. He got it from a tribal elder there. The elder had lost three sons trying to control it and was more than glad to be rid of it.'

As if to illustrate Scrabsnitch's point, the carpet made another low pass over them before punching its way straight through the back of the leather armchair he had been sitting on only moments before.

'Good Lord,' Morris shouted. 'How are we going to stop it from taking our heads off?'

'We were much younger men when Bonehill and I managed to tie it up tight,' Scrabsnitch panted. 'And even then he got a broken arm for his pains. It's been bound up for years. I wouldn't recommend getting in its way now.'

'We can't just lie down here,' Ness snapped, jumping up and then throwing herself flat on the floor again. The air snapped by her ear as the thing shot past her. 'Then again, maybe we can.'

'If you distract it,' Azuli whispered to Morris and Ness, 'then I can jump on it and pin it down.'

'Don't be ridiculous, sonny,' Morris grunted. 'There's nothing of you; it'll throw you off in an instant.'

The carpet hurtled around the emporium, whipping books from the shelves and sending them crashing to the floor.

'It's just like old times,' Scrabsnitch muttered, watching his shop being destroyed. 'But I really am too old for this now.'

'I'm going for it,' Azuli yelled and sprang up, grabbing hold of the carpet as it flew over him. For a moment he hung in the air, the look of terror on his face almost comical. Ness gasped as the carpet veered left and sent him smacking into a bookshelf and tumbling to the floor under a pile of heavy, leather-bound tomes.

The carpet executed another fly-by just as Azuli struggled, dazed, to his feet. Ness screamed a warning. It would cut him in half if she didn't do something. With a yell, Ness leapt up on to the cabinets that filled the middle of the room, running along their frames, desperate not to put her feet through the glass. The carpet flew close; Ness could see the rough weave rippling like black flames. She threw herself at it, gripping the sides and tucking her legs into herself so she knelt on the carpet.

It felt strange underneath her; warm and alive but slightly unpleasant. Ness had ridden horses at the Academy, had enjoyed their strength and that feeling of oneness as they rode together. But this wasn't like that at all. It was powerful, yes, but grudging, malevolent. She could almost smell the carpet's desire to throw her off and crush every bone in her body.

Feeling Ness's weight, the carpet swirled upside down, its corners snapping and whipping at her face. Ness kept her grip as she felt gravity drag at her body. Her shoulders and waist ached as she struggled to keep her body in a tight ball. Her knuckles cracked as she gripped the coarse fabric. The carpet righted itself, then performed a series of rippling bucks. Still Ness held on.

The room spun around, a dangling chandelier scraped her back and then crashed to the floor. Bookshelves and suits of armour rushed by in a dizzying circle. Bile rose in Ness's throat as the carpet somersaulted and weaved in and out of the cabinets, trying to dislodge her.

Morris's alarmed face went flashing by them at one point. Then she heard Azuli calling out.

'Ness, jump! It's going to . . .'

Ness's eyes widened as the carpet flew straight for the shop windows.

If wishes were horses, beggars would ride.

Traditional proverb

CHAPTER TWENTY-ONE
MAGIC CARPET RIDE

Gritting her teeth, Ness dragged at the edges of the carpet, using them as a shield as they hit the glass. The sound of splintering wood and shattering glass deafened her. Cold air hit her face as the crowd in the street screamed at the sudden appearance of Ness and the carpet.

Hats and white faces flashed past her, then the dilapidated brickwork of the shops on the other side of Jesmond Street were quickly replaced by roof tiles rushing by. Ness's stomach lurched as the carpet increased speed. The smoke and smog of the city choked her as the carpet whisked her above the rooftops. She screwed her eyes shut, her fingers aching as she gripped tighter.

Higher and higher they flew. Ness panted for breath in the freezing air. For a moment she hung weightless. She opened her eyes and stared in amazement. The whole of London sprawled below her. Straight-line bridges crossed the river, which was dotted with tiny ships as it wriggled its way into the distance. Church spires poked up above the slates and chimneys. A thick, sulphurous yellow fog clung to the south bank, where factories, tanneries and workshops clanked and pounded out their wares. Ness glimpsed the Houses of Parliament, the dome of St Paul's, streets intersecting each other and running into wide squares.

Ness almost let go but then the carpet began its descent. Closer the rooftops hurtled, the wind whipping her face. The city spiralled and careered towards them and Ness felt a cry of exultation forcing its way out of her heart. She didn't care if she died. She didn't care what happened. She wasn't afraid of anything.

'D'you hear me, you scrappy old rag?' she screamed as the slates and chimneys, the bricks and coping stones came rushing towards her. 'You can never beat me!' Ness tugged at the weave of the carpet. Did she feel it flinch? She dug her nails into the ropy fabric. 'And you must do as I say! Now take me back to the emporium!'

Apparently sensing a worthy adversary, the carpet flew up again, narrowly missing the shop roofs, skimming archways and gateways, making Ness both curse at the carpet and cackle like a witch at the screams of pedestrians they nearly mowed down.

Gradually they circled closer to Jesmond Street and the carpet whisked her back through the jagged window and stopped abruptly in front of the gaping Morris, Scrabsnitch and Azuli.

Ness jumped off, just managing to land on her feet but keeping tight hold of the carpet.

'Rope, quickly!' she panted. Morris threw her the rope and she tied one end loosely around the middle of the carpet and the other around the leg of an upended display cabinet. The carpet tugged and shuddered against the rope but was tamed for the moment.

'Are you all right, Ness?' Morris spluttered.

'Never better, why?' Ness grinned, still catching her breath.

'What did you do?' Azuli said, staring at the carpet warily.

'Just showed it who's boss, that's all,' she said, putting her hands on her hips. 'Now, these papers of my father's, where are they?'

All afternoon, they pored over the dusty documents that lay scattered on the floor – diaries, scrolls from ancient civilisations, maps – but nothing told them more than they already knew.

'The bloodstone,' Ness whispered, holding up an illustration torn from some long-forgotten book. The picture showed a hooded figure holding a glowing red stone above his head. Strange, horned creatures – half man, half beast – seemed to be being sucked into the stone in the figure's hand.

'The what?' Azuli said, pulling a face.

'The bloodstone,' Scrabsnitch murmured. 'A legendary gem that is said to be capable of finding spirits or demons, even unfortunate mortal souls. It is said that with the right incantation a bloodstone can imprison anything. Anthony became obsessed with finding it after Grossford took the bottle away. He searched for it for years.'

'I remember it from home,' Ness whispered, staring intently at the picture. 'He had a bloodstone set into a ring. Is it valuable?'

'Only to those who know how to use it. It's a mere bauble otherwise,' Scrabsnitch replied, running his gnarled fingers through his frizzy grey hair. 'I never heard of him trying to catch a demon with it. Maybe he thought it would protect him against the possible return of the djinn.'

Ness found her thoughts drawn back to her father's study. The ring lying on the desk. His voice booming in her mind. *'Take it, try it on. You love the bloodstone, don't you? It's beautiful. One day it will be all yours.'*

'It doesn't seem to have helped him,' Morris grunted, snapping Ness from her daydream. He sat some distance away, polishing the blunderbuss and oiling the firing mechanism. He jumped up, staring at the floor as his feet scrunched through broken glass.

'No.' Scrabsnitch shook his head. 'If Anthony had bound the djinn into the ring then your father would be here now. I do hope Anthony and Eliza are all right.'

'So do I,' Ness murmured.

'What's this, Scrabsnitch?' Morris said, scooping up a handful of shining metal from the debris on the floor.

'Do you want the truth?' Scrabsnitch reddened a little. 'It was labelled as part of a hoard of Druid silver but it's actually just some melted sixpences.'

'But silver, yes?' Morris grunted.

Scrabsnitch nodded and Morris poured it into the barrel of the blunderbuss.

'This is useless,' Azuli groaned, slapping a map down on the floor. The flying carpet bucked and rippled at the noise. 'We don't even know what we're looking for!'

'Anything that might give us a clue as to how to destroy this djinn,' Ness said, whistling through her teeth with frustration.

'Is this silver?' Morris muttered, showing another handful of metal to Scrabsnitch, who looked shamefaced and shook his head. Morris cursed and threw it down.

'The sword,' Azuli muttered, rubbing his face. 'That was the only hope. And I lost it.'

Morris sat some distance away, making no comment as he laboriously scraped at the metal he had retrieved before.

'Where do the djinns come from, Mr Scrabsnitch?' Ness asked.

'According to ancient wisdom, they are creations of God, just like men,' Scrabsnitch said, stroking his beard. 'But djinns are creatures of powerful magic. God is said to have made them first, before Adam. Some say that they lived in the Garden of Eden before mankind.' The old man paused and rummaged through a pile of scrolls until he found a particular one and passed it to Ness.

'*A djinn can choose his way*,' she read aloud. '*He can worship God or Satan, himself or nobody. The djinns are powerful but can be bound to vessels and objects by trickery or obligation*. What does that mean?'

Scrabsnitch shrugged. 'Sometimes a djinn can be arrogant or ignorant and will enter a magic vessel just to prove it can or because it doesn't know the danger. Or it can be bound if it feels it has to save a loved one or because it *should* obey.'

'How could we trick Zaakiel?' Ness wondered aloud.

'Zaakiel is very old,' Azuli said from the shadows of the shop. 'He would not be tricked easily and he has no love for any living thing.'

'A-ha!' Scrabsnitch shouted, making Ness jump. 'That's it! Necessity, you are a genius.'

'I am?'

'Yes.' Scrabsnitch beamed, holding open a thick book with heavy, yellowed pages. 'When you asked where the djinns come from, it awakened a memory. A memory of a place.'

'A place?' Azuli frowned, drawn back to them by the outburst.

'The oldest of places, the only remaining part of the original garden,' explained Scrabsnitch. 'The place where all things were first made. The Oasis of the Amarant.'

'The Amarant?' Azuli said. 'What is that?'

'A mythical bloom full of power and tragedy,' Scrabsnitch said, scanning the pages of the book. 'It was fed by waters from the Pool of Life.'

'How will this Amarant help us?' Ness said, confused.

'The Amarant is long gone but the Pool of Life remains deep within the oasis,' Scrabsnitch said, pointing to a page. 'It is said to give all the answers a seeker would need about his life. But the pool is guarded. Only the brave need go there.'

'And do you know for certain that this oasis exists?' Azuli said, frowning.

'Some colleagues of mine went there many years ago,' Scrabsnitch said. 'I still have the maps.'

'Could they guide us there again?' Ness said.

Scrabsnitch shook his head slowly. 'Alas, no,' he sighed. 'Their contact with the oasis did not end well.'

'Marvellous,' Azuli groaned. 'And I assume that the oasis isn't in this country?'

Scrabsnitch was on the move again, scrabbling through cupboards and throwing papers right and left as he searched. Finally he pulled a map from the back of an old chest.

'No, it's in Abyssinia,' he said, his face lighting up. 'Here is Mortlock's map.'

'Mortlock?' Ness frowned. 'One of your old friends?'

'You've missed one thing, Mr Scrabsnitch,' Azuli said, shaking his head. 'It would take us weeks, months even, to get there.'

Scrabsnitch caught Ness's eye, then looked sidelong at the flying carpet, flicking its corners and rippling waspishly. He held out the map. 'You could be there and back in no time at all. What an uncanny piece of luck that Azuli freed the carpet.'

'I think your luck just ran out,' hissed a voice from the shattered windows.

A cloud of noxious, green mist boiled into the emporium, solidifying into the form of a much more robust djinn. Ness's mouth felt dry and she swallowed hard. Zaakiel's wrist stump still bled but muscles now rippled under his leprous skin. His topknot of hair swung over his shoulder. His manic grin still split his skeletal face.

'I knew you'd come eventually,' Scrabsnitch sighed. 'But I'm not quite as resigned to dying as I was, having met these lovely young people.'

Azuli lurched forward, slashing with his sword. It passed through Zaakiel as if he were made of smoke.

'Hmm, a miraculous recovery, little boy. You want to be careful with sharp blades,' Zaakiel smirked, shaking his gory wrist stump, 'or you'll have someone's arm off – but not with that toothpick.'

He swung his good hand, sending Azuli crashing back into the wrecked armchair.

'Well, try this for size. Each piece of silver has a little Z carved on it in your honour,' Morris said, stepping from behind a suit of armour, firing the blunderbuss at Zaakiel at almost point-blank range.

The enormous, roaring explosion filled the emporium and Morris was lifted off his feet. The djinn was lost in a hail of silver. With a howl of anguish, he spiralled up into the room and crashed through the ceiling, bloody furrows carving his face and body. Plaster and splinters of wood came crashing down from the hole he left.

'If you're going to get that carpet moving, Ness, you'd better do it now,' Morris yelled, pouring more gunpowder down the barrel and stuffing some wadding and then more shards of silver after it.

'But I can't leave you,' Ness argued.

'You can do more good by going to the oasis,' Scrabsnitch snapped. 'D'you want to die here or stop the djinn?'

'We can keep him occupied here.' Morris grinned. A trickle of blood oozed down his brow. 'If we can, we'll join the Lashkars. Old Zaakiel here will be picking shrapnel from his backside for a week!'

At the mention of his name, the djinn came howling back from above. Morris pursed his lips, his moustache bristling, and squeezed the trigger again. Once more the deafening bang made Ness's ears ring. And once more Zaakiel screamed his rage. The blast sent him across the shop, crashing into a huge stuffed grizzly bear. Shards of silver poked from the djinn's body, sizzling where they had embedded themselves.

Snatching the map from Scrabsnitch, Ness tucked it into the waistband of her trousers and jumped on to the carpet, which shivered and skipped about. She untied the rope and the carpet began to rise.

'I'll be as quick as I can,' Ness cried as she floated higher above their heads.

'Wait!' Azuli picked himself up, bounded on to a squat display cabinet, jumped up the side of a tumbled-down cupboard and leapt on to the back of the carpet. The carpet jerked, nearly dislodging Ness. The carpet flew out of the emporium and up into the darkening sky.

Ness bit her lip as another thunderous boom echoed below, then they slipped high above the sounds of London, leaving Morris and Scrabsnitch to their fate.

Part the Third

The Oasis of the Amarant

She who wishes to travel far spares her steed.

Traditional proverb

CHAPTER TWENTY-TWO

SKY VOYAGE

The carpet hurtled skyward until London became indistinct and the air smelt sweet then became very thin. Ness shook her head. Azuli lay on the back of the carpet, face down, his knuckles white from holding on to the edges.

'Down,' Ness gasped, scraping her nails into the fibres of the rug. 'I know what you're trying to do and it's not on! Down, now!'

The carpet pointed nose first and flew down, forcing Ness to lean back against Azuli. She could feel his weight pushing her off the carpet. His constant screams of terror didn't help either.

'If you carry on like this,' Ness yelled at the carpet, yanking the edges cruelly, 'then I'll land you in a volcano and you can burn for all I care!'

The carpet levelled out, giving a surly flick every now and then. Azuli scrambled behind Ness and sat up, still gripping the edges tight. The freezing wind battered her face and tore the cap from her head. Ness tried to pull the map from her waistband. It flapped about in her hands, then blew away completely.

'Hold on,' Ness yelled and tugged on the carpet's edge, forcing it to double back.

The map danced madly in the wind but Ness forced the carpet towards it until it fluttered above their heads.

'Grab it,' Ness called to Azuli, but he was frozen to the carpet.

Ness flailed one hand out and snagged the map just as the carpet sensed its chance. She gave a scream as the carpet flipped to the left, sending her off the edge and dangling on by one aching arm. Azuli stared at her in terror, his fingers firmly wrapped around the edge as the carpet twisted and turned. Ness thought her arm would come out of its socket and her head felt like a sack full of iron as it was dragged back with the velocity.

'Right, that's it,' she snarled, releasing the map to its fate. She slapped her flailing hand back on to the carpet, twisting her fingers into the weave once more. Another desperate heave brought her back on top of the carpet but not before she'd managed to kick Azuli on the nose.

Ness ground her teeth and rage boiled in her stomach as she drove the carpet straight towards the ground. The landscape became more open, with fields and trees. Then hedgerows and a few branches were visible. Then individual tree trunks.

'Ness! What are you doing?' Azuli screamed.

'Calling its bluff!' Ness yelled back.

The ground came rushing towards them. Ness could feel the wind slapping her face. Azuli's horrified scream deafened her. The carpet tried to veer upward again. Clearly it didn't want to hit the ground any more than she did. At the last moment, Ness dragged the carpet upward, long stems of grass whipping at them as they grazed the earth.

'If you want to crash,' Ness snapped at the carpet, 'just let me know. I'll arrange it. Now, I reckon you know where we're going. Take us to the Oasis of the Amarant!'

'You're mad,' Azuli said, laughing, sobbing and trying to suck in huge mouthfuls of air all at once.

'Barking.' Ness grinned back, wild-eyed.

They both laughed as they careered across the twilight sky.

Ness woke with a start, half expecting to find herself falling, thrown to her death by the rogue carpet. She and Azuli huddled together as best they could, trying to fend off the bitter chill. If only she'd had time to put on a coat or something warmer. She didn't remember dozing off. The carpet had settled into a steady flight pattern, only bumping occasionally. *I wonder if the carpet is asleep too*.

A wave of tired sadness washed over Ness and she tried not to think of the besieged Lashkars or Morris and

Scrabsnitch. She thought instead of her father. *Why did he search so hard for the bloodstone? Had he hoped to trap the djinn with it if Uncle Carlos freed it? And what about Mama? What did she wish for?* She thought of her father's wish. The Lashkars and Scrabsnitch both suggested he'd wished for great wealth because a few months later, her grandparents had died, leaving a fortune to her mother. *Did he really make that wish? Did he know that would happen? Mama would have hated him for it.*

Stars glowed, dusted across the dark-blue sky. Down below waves lashed white against a black shoreline. *What country is this?* Ness wondered. The distant, curved horizon grew yellow, waking the purple tops of densely packed mountains.

Day five, Ness thought.

Azuli stirred as they travelled into daylight and thin wisps of cloud. He gave a start and grabbed Ness's shoulder. He too was shocked to find he had slept.

'It's fine,' Ness shouted, placing a reassuring hand over his. 'We're safe.' Their eyes met and Ness's hand lingered just a moment before she snatched it away.

Azuli shook himself and peered over the side of the carpet. 'Where are we?' he said, his voice loud above the whistling wind that tousled their hair.

'I don't know,' Ness shouted back, looking at the ever-changing landscape. 'Not England, for sure. Look.'

She pointed down at the brown earth below. The whole landscape looked parched. The odd scrubby clump of trees and bushes clung to the barren hillsides but little seemed to live in this world.

'Everything looks dead,' Azuli said. The carpet gave a menacing flicker, making him grip the edge tightly.

Ness gave a hiss and dug her nails into the carpet. 'Don't you dare,' she snarled. 'Woken up, have you?'

The carpet gave a few rebellious shudders but kept a steady path.

The ground below drifted by, unchanging. Now and then, a small herd of deer slipped beneath them. Ness swore she saw a caravan of camels but it was hard to tell. The ground became monotonous and unreal.

'At least we're warm now,' she called to Azuli, who grinned back.

But her mirth wore off as they flew on. The sun blazed down, scorching her arms and head. Ness tried talking to Azuli to distract herself from her thirst.

'How old were you when Taimur took you in?' she asked.

'Three or four, I believe,' Azuli replied. 'I can't remember much before that.'

'Do you remember when the other children were banished?'

Azuli shook his head. 'No, I was taken in by the Lashkars about nine or ten years after the banishment. They tell the story almost every day though. It is so sad. They fought a fierce djinn called Amoteth. He had slain those who freed him and it took the full might of the Lashkars to subdue him. Jabalah himself wielded the sword. Seeing the finishing blow coming his way, Amoteth cursed Jabalah's son, all his generation and any dear to them. They simply vanished – the young men, their wives, the grandchildren. Gone.'

'That's terrible,' Ness gasped.

'Yes, but clever too because it destroyed the Lashkars as a fighting force. Only the old remain. Hafid believes their children are trapped in the same way the djinns were, in a bottle or a jewel or some other item. It is a burden those left behind carry always.'

Ness nodded back but felt too exhausted to continue the conversation. The long, hot day wore on. Her mouth felt thick and dry. The desiccating wind blew hot on her face.

'We need water,' Azuli croaked, salty sweat caked on his forehead.

The earth below glared white, dazzling them and reflecting its heat upwards. Ness's head pounded and whiteness filled her vision. Her lips felt rough and cracked. She screwed up her stinging face against the wind. Bile rose in her throat.

The carpet suddenly lurched downward, making Ness grip the rippling edges. The white earth blinded her but a small spot of black in the distance slowly became a disc of green, then a wreath of shivering leaves.

The carpet wasn't slowing down. The oasis grew larger and larger. For a second, it filled Ness's failing vision, then branches whipped at her face, tore at her hair. Somewhere

Azuli yelled and the carpet rose as his weight vanished behind Ness.

'Azuli!' Ness screamed, groping about the carpet hoping to grab him but she had to keep her eyes shut tight for fear of being blinded by the passing trees. Azuli's cry faded, growing more distant as he fell.

Ness tugged at the carpet's front, pulling it up again. For a few brief seconds they flew up and down, veering this way and that as she wrestled for control. Blinding sunlight forced Ness's eyes shut again as they broke clear of the oasis, then Ness swung her weight to the left, forcing the carpet into a mad downward spiral. The brown desert earth came hurtling towards them and Ness braced herself for the impact. But the carpet also feared such a crash, it seemed, as at the last moment it slowed and skimmed along the hot sand. Even then the stop was abrupt enough to send Ness rolling forward. Her grip on the carpet didn't loosen so it tangled around her, shielding her body.

With a groan, Ness rolled on to her hands and knees pinning the carpet. 'You poor excuse for a hearthrug! Why can't you –'

She stopped as she was gazing down on a pair of brown, scuffed boots. The laces had long gone and holes gaped in the leather. Ness lifted her gaze from the boots up to the legs that stood before her. Brown socks to the knees, skinny, tanned and grazed. Then khaki shorts, a thick leather belt and a ragged shirt stuffed inside. Bony hands rested on the belt as the man stared down at her with a lopsided grin. The man's whole face seemed crooked; his nose, his teeth, even his eyes seemed to look slightly to one side of her.

'Well, well,' he said, scratching his dirty fingers over his stubbly chin. 'What 'ave we 'ere?'

TRUST THE DOG AND THE WOLF SLIPS INTO THE SHEEPFOLD.

TRADITIONAL PROVERB

CHAPTER TWENTY-THREE

THE CORPORAL

Ness dragged herself to her feet, keeping the carpet firmly pinned under one boot, and glanced around.

'Azuli? Where's he gone?' she stammered, panic welling up inside her. 'I must find him . . . I can't lose him . . . It'll be my fault and . . .'

She shaded her eyes and scanned the barren desert landscape. Packages and boxes lay empty and strewn about them. A fire smouldered within a ring of stones in front of a tent that billowed slightly in the faint breeze. Behind her, the green wall of the oasis reared up, menacing and impenetrable.

'Two of yer, eh?' the man said, his voice hoarse from years in the desert. 'With a flyin' carpet an' all. Well, this is a turn up for the books an' no mistake. Do you 'ave a name, girl?'

'What? Oh, sorry. Necessity.' Ness gave a nod but continued to gaze into the oasis as if Azuli would pop up above it like a jack-in-the-box. 'Necessity Bonehill.'

The man stood to attention, stamping his foot and giving a quivering salute which made Ness jump. 'Corporal Rusty Grubb, Fourth Hinderton Rifles, at your service, miss!' he yelled, then he squinted one eye at her. 'Bonehill, y'say? I knew a Bonehill once . . .'

Ness's head still throbbed. She stopped scanning the treeline and turned to stare at the ragged soldier. 'Did you say Hinderton Rifles?' Ness croaked.

'You know of them?' Grubb stepped forward excitedly.

'My father was –'

'Captain Anthony Bonehill,' Grubb finished for her. He shook her hand vigorously. 'I had the, er, the . . . pleasure of servin' under him in the Hindu Kush.' Ness noticed his eye wander down to the carpet.

'Corporal,' Ness sobbed, swaying slightly. 'I've got to find my friend. I don't know if he's alive or . . .'

'Don't worry, miss,' Corporal Grubb said, gripping Ness's shoulder and steadying her. 'We'll search for 'im but you need a drink first. There's plenty of daylight left. But if he's in there,' Grubb gave a sidelong glance at the gloom of the oasis, 'well, there's not much 'ope.'

Corporal Grubb disappeared inside his tent for a moment and returned with a canteen full of water.

'Drink as much as you want, miss. Plenty more coming soon,' he said, giving a crooked grin. 'It'll revive yer good an' proper, no mistake!'

Ness gratefully poured the water into her mouth and over her face, gasping at how good it tasted and felt. It woke her up. Even her aches from wrestling with the carpet faded. Suddenly Ness felt strong.

She looked down at the ragged black mass that rippled under her foot. Ness fell to her knees and gripped the carpet with both hands. It writhed and squirmed in her grip as she rolled it as tightly as she could.

'Do you have any rope, Corporal?' she panted, squashing her fists down on the wriggling roll.

The Corporal glanced about his campsite and seemed to wilt. Ness followed his gaze, frowning. Now she had a proper chance to look at it, the place looked as though it had been ransacked. Crates lay tipped on their sides, empty sacks draped over them, here and there a barrel poked out of the sand, and Ness could see the remains of other tents collapsed and half buried. She thought of Sergeant Major Morris's cluttered but orderly cottage. The only thing the Corporal and Morris appeared to have in common was a khaki uniform. Grubb's jawline seemed to waver with indecision whereas Morris's jutted out defiantly; his shoulders sloped where Morris's were square. Grubb was a broken man, as far as Ness could see.

'I'm on me own now,' the Corporal said in a low voice, stroking his palm over his balding head. 'Can't keep the place as shipshape as I'd like.' He gave a cough and straightened his back. 'Anyway,' he said, raising his voice and striding over to one of the submerged tents and rummaging in the sand. 'I think I might 'ave something better.' He stood up and revealed a belt with a flourish that reminded Ness of a conjuror. 'It belonged to one of my boys.' Grubb looked away. 'He . . . Well, he don't need it now.'

Ness wrapped the belt around the carpet and yanked it tight, buckling it and slamming a wooden crate over the whole lot just for good measure. She looked up and saw Grubb scurrying towards the edge of the oasis.

'You don't seem very surprised by my appearance,' Ness called, catching up with him. 'Or by the carpet, for that matter.'

Grubb gave a twisted grin full of crooked teeth. 'I'm a corporal in the Fourth Hinderton Rifles,' he said. 'I've seen most things. You learn to not be surprised by anything.'

'How did you end up here?' Ness asked, taking a moment to stare around at the desert. The edge of the oasis was to their left. Thin tree trunks crushed close together, shaded by green leaves. Even in the narrow shadows between the trees, Ness thought she could see movement.

Grubb gave a sigh. 'I told you. I'm a soldier. The Fourth Hindertons are special though.' He stopped. '*Were* special. I don't suppose there's many of us left now, if any.'

'Why not?' Ness said.

The Corporal seemed to shudder. 'It's an old story,' he muttered, glancing into the shadows. 'As the British empire grew, us soldiers found ourselves in stranger and stranger lands. Sometimes we were up against . . . Well, let's just say against things that shouldn't exist. It's a big world and there's more in it than we understand.'

'So the Hinderton Rifles were formed to fight these . . . things?' Ness said.

Grubb turned suddenly and grabbed Ness's hands. 'Demons, monsters, wraiths and ghosts, bloodsuckers and night crawlers!' he gabbled, his eyes wide. 'I've seen 'em all. Killed 'em all. Seen me mates killed by 'em.' He stopped and shook his head. 'The bloodsuckers are the worst – they change people . . .'

'I . . . I'm sorry,' Ness murmured, easing her hands out of his cold grasp. She remembered Morris's sometimes strange, haunted behaviour. She didn't know why but she didn't want to mention Morris to this man. 'So what brought you here?'

'The Amarant.' Grubb's eyes glowed. 'We were an expeditionary force sent into the desert to find this oasis. To find it and destroy it if we could.'

'Destroy it? Why?'

'It's a place of mischief and evil,' Grubb said, shaking. 'It was our mission to go in and cut the trees down, every one, raze the place to the ground. Fifty men came 'ere.'

'Fifty men?' Ness echoed. 'And you're the only one left?'

Grubb looked down, licked his lips. 'We sent party after party into the oasis. The trees just swallowed them up. They never came out again – well, not all of 'em.'

'What do you mean?' Ness frowned.

'Oh, listen to me,' Grubb said, his voice a little too loud, a little too cheery. 'All doom and gloom. Wastin' time telling horror stories. We'd better find that pal of yours quick time!'

'Right, come on,' Ness said, dragging back the branches at the fringe of the oasis.

Grubb caught her elbow. 'I wouldn't recommend actually goin' in,' he muttered, craning his neck and squinting his eyes.

'But I can't just waste my time wandering around the edge,' Ness snapped. 'Azuli could be injured in there.'

'You go in and you'll be lost in a second, dead in a minute,' Grubb hissed.

'What's in there that's so dangerous?' Ness said, pursing her lips. 'You started to tell me but then clammed up.'

Grubb flinched a little and then settled on an old tree trunk that was white and bleached by the sun. 'They say that all this round 'ere used to be the Garden of Eden.' Grubb swung his hand slowly over his head. 'Until the good Lord took it all away up to heaven. But one little bit was left behind, see.'

'Yes, I've heard that before,' Ness said, screwing up her face to stare around at the desiccated scenery.

'Trouble is, so I'm told, this 'ere oasis is so soaked in ancient magic that it became like a magnet, drawing all kinds of strange things from the spirit world. Ghosties and ghouls and the like.' Grubb's voice was little more than a whisper and Ness shivered despite the blazing heat. 'They can't resist it, y'see. Drawn to it like moths to a candle flame. It's like a gateway. An outlet where all manner of fiend and afrit comes a-tumblin' into the real world. So, I'm sorry to say that if your friend is in there, he don't stand a chance against 'em.'

They wandered along the edge of the oasis for what seemed like hours. Grubb would squint into the shadows from the brightness of the desert, wary of even stepping into the shade cast by the trees. From time to time he would pick up a broken branch and poke it gingerly into the undergrowth but he wouldn't venture any further. Ness would barge forward only to be yanked back.

'I'm tellin' yer, it's suicide to go any deeper,' Grubb whined.

'I won't give up on him,' Ness finally declared, stamping back towards the camp. 'I have the carpet – I can fly over, search for him that way.'

Into the late afternoon, Ness flew back and forth, criss-crossing the oasis, peering into its depths. Sometimes she thought she saw something shift or squirm in the darkness beneath the leaves, but she never saw any sign of Azuli. At times, she hovered, dragging back the uppermost branches of the trees and calling his name into the emptiness below. No birds sang, no animals roared. All stayed silent and Azuli did not call back.

Ness felt hollow and empty. She had found the Oasis of the Amarant but all she could think of was Azuli. She bit her lip and swallowed hard.

Lowering the carpet beneath the canopy, Ness peered to the ground. It was like being underwater; a blue shadow tinted everything. How could a place that once sustained the Amarant feel so desolate and deathly silent?

The shadows grew darker, forcing Ness up and out of the oasis. Evening was coming. She gave a final shout and a sigh before turning the carpet back towards Grubb's camp.

A fire crackled outside his tent by the time Ness returned. The flames wobbled, casting long shadows and making Grubb's face seem even more twisted. He squatted, warming his knobbly fingers over the flames.

'No luck?' he said as Ness sat opposite him, binding the belt around the carpet.

'No,' she said, staring into the flames. The darkness surrounded them and Ness felt as if the sphere of flickering light was all that remained of the world. She picked up the canteen and drank deeply. Then she stopped and frowned, holding the container up to the light. 'Where do you get water from?'

Grubb looked at her across the fire. 'Funny you should ask,' he said, settling himself on his haunches. 'And it's a bit of a story. We came 'ere ten years ago. All one hundred of us. We lost a few on the way, as yer do.'

'You said fifty before! You lost half your men just getting here?' Ness frowned.

'These are cruel lands,' Corporal Grubb said, giving a lopsided grin that faded as he continued. 'The first group of twenty who went into the oasis just didn't come out again. Never saw 'em, never knew what happened to 'em. The captain and a couple of men went in to find 'em.' The shadows seemed to shift around them. Ness could hear the sound of sand sifting through something; a hissing, shushing noise. Grubb continued, apparently unconcerned. 'The captain came back this time. He was different though. Changed.'

Ness looked from left to right. The ground seemed to be moving under her. She jumped up. 'What's happening?' she demanded.

Grubb stared at her. 'I watched 'im drain the blood from every last man 'ere and they all changed in turn. Then he came to me.'

A pale hand punched up through the sand to Ness's left, then another to her right. Behind Grubb, a figure in torn khaki heaved itself from the ground as the sand around it sank into the space beneath. A young man, tall with a thin beard over his pointed chin. His hair was long, slicked back. His skin was leprous white, lined and dry. He grinned, sharp teeth glinting in the firelight.

'But he let me live, see.' Grubb turned to face the creature. 'Got yer another one, captain, sir.' He saluted.

More figures dragged themselves from the sand.

'I find them blood, they get me water from the pool. Easy, really. Sorry an' all but it's me or you. I'm sure yer understand.'

Truth is brighter than the light,
Falsehood darker than the night.

'Riddles Wisely Expounded', traditional folk ballad

CHAPTER TWENTY-FOUR

THE POOL

The bloodsuckers stood all around Grubb now, leering at Ness. She could see that they had been ordinary men once, soldiers in khaki. The remnants of their uniforms hung from their pale bodies. But their faces looked harsh, pointed in nose and chin. Cruel fangs filled their mouths and sharp talons tipped their long fingers. At the front stood the younger man, their captain, his sinewy arms folded as he appraised Ness with greedy, crimson eyes.

'I don't enjoy it,' Corporal Grubb said, his voice almost apologetic. 'But I was dyin' of thirst first time 'e came to me. See, they can't live without blood an' the daylight kills 'em. They can live in that dark oasis fer a bit but they 'as to go underground eventually. They needed me. Made a deal, we did. That water from the pool, it lasts for months, never goes green. You'd be amazed 'ow many folks come lookin' for this place even now.'

'You're a monster,' Ness hissed, edging backward to the wooden crate.

The carpet rattled and bucked inside as if it sensed the danger and wanted to get away too.

The captain gave a low chuckle and took a step, signalling to two of the other bloodsuckers. The pair loped forward, reaching out for Ness. She ducked beneath the arms of one and kicked the legs out from under the other. The bloodsucker howled as he tumbled backward into the fire. Flames licked their way up his bone-dry clothes, consuming his desiccated flesh. Howling, the creature stumbled off into the night.

But the other swung round and grabbed Ness about her neck. Ness could smell the creature's rank breath on her cheek; feel his cold, dry skin against hers. She kicked back at him as the captain advanced, flanked by the remaining soldiers. Ness flipped herself forward, doubling up and sending the creature behind sailing over her head. Without pausing, she kicked over the crate that held the carpet. The carpet bounced off the ground, still held by the leather belt. Ness pounced on it, fumbling at the buckle. Cold hands grabbed at her, pulling her back. Ness punched out, trying to get the belt free, but her stomach lurched as she was dragged to her feet.

She was held now, a soldier at each elbow, gripping her tight. The captain stepped towards her, laughing as Ness lashed out with her feet. The firelight glowed on his white cheek as he opened his mouth close to hers.

Then he stopped.

'What's this?' he hissed, pulling back from Ness's neck and staring at Grubb.

'What d'you mean?' Grubb rubbed his hands together and scurried forward. 'She's a girl. A human girl. I couldn't 'ave got a better feast for you if I'd chosen her meself!'

'She's not for us,' hissed the captain, turning on Grubb.

'Not fer you?' Grubb whined. 'I don't understand . . . I . . .' His eyes widened as the soldiers dropped Ness and started to pace towards him.

'She's not for us,' the captain repeated. 'But we hunger.'

Ness didn't wait to watch. She threw herself down again, gripping the carpet with one hand and freeing the belt with the other. The carpet flapped open, rippling for a second. She pulled herself up on to the front. Something snagged it as it took off. Ness glanced at the weight that had suddenly thrown itself on to her back.

'Don't let them get me,' Grubb sobbed as he gripped on to her hair, the carpet – anything to stop him from slipping.

'Don't! You're pulling me down,' Ness hissed. Her fingers slid along the carpet as Grubb tried to scrabble over her.

'They'll kill me,' he sobbed, slipping slightly. 'I don't want to be like them.'

But the carpet had other ideas. With a flick and a twist, it sent Grubb sailing downward. Ness couldn't pull her gaze from his startled face as he dwindled down towards the pale figures around the firelight below. With a gentle thump and a cloud of ashes, Grubb hit the ground, landing by the fire. Ness squeezed her eyes shut as the pack of bloodsuckers threw themselves at the twitching body, but not quite in time to blot out the image of flame licking across Grubb's uniform and the fountain of red that hissed in the heat of the fire.

Something whipped her face. Ness opened her eyes but could only see the darkness of the oasis. The carpet had flown straight into the canopy of trees.

'You did that on purpose,' Ness snarled, yanking at the front.

But they were already deep into the jungle. Branches and creepers tore at Ness, wrapping around her and threatening to drag her off the carpet. Briars ripped at her cheek. A thick overhanging branch loomed in front of her. Ness forced the carpet beneath it but her shoulder glanced off another limb that protruded from the great tree trunk.

A sickening stab of pain lanced up her neck and down her side as her arm flapped free, broken like a straw and now being buffeted by the foliage around her. The trees pulled and tore at her hair. The carpet twisted over as if wringing itself out and, with a scream, Ness plunged down, bouncing off branches and ripping through thorns until the leafy ground rose up to meet her.

The impact forced every breath of air from Ness's body. The crack of ribs and the thud of her weight on the earth filled her ears. She curled up, writhing in silent agony on the ground until, not caring what happened next, she let herself slip into unconsciousness.

*

How long Ness lay there, she wasn't sure. She opened her eyes a crack. Bile filled her throat, forcing her to roll over and vomit into the soft, mossy ground. Her whole body throbbed with pain. Her ribs, her arm and shoulder all pulsed agonisingly. The canopy she had fallen through allowed only a few ghostly shafts of sunlight through. It was daytime, then. She tried to sit up but pain burned in her shoulder and she fell back, groaning. Flies danced in and out of the pillars of grey light. She realised that she lay in a clearing; the thick jungle formed a wall that circled her.

Something thrashed around above her head. Ness squinted up. An indistinct silhouette wriggled and twisted as if trapped up in the canopy. Then a closer sound made her heart pound. Footsteps breaking through the undergrowth. Ness grunted, trying to get up, but fell back wincing. Nausea pressed at her throat again. Her arm lay useless at her side, throbbing with pain. The cracking of twigs grew louder. *I'm helpless*, she thought.

The sound came nearer. Gritting her teeth, Ness pushed up with her good arm. Her ribs burned and her shattered arm swung like an excruciating pendulum. Gasping with every move, she managed to stagger to her feet. The clearing tipped and swung around as she struggled to stay upright. With a moan, she staggered backward, trying to keep her footing, but the ground vanished from under her and she felt herself falling.

The cold hit her. Icy, wet. She glimpsed a figure emerging from the shadows but then the black water she had stumbled into engulfed her, roaring in her ears as she sank beneath the surface.

For a second Ness felt weightless. Her pain receded and the freezing water revived her. *Freezing? How can that be?* Even in the gloomy clearing, the heat had been unbearable.

Ness kicked her legs, amazed at the lack of pain. She sliced at the water with her good arm and instinctively brought up her other arm. *No pain! No break!* Although underwater, she opened her eyes to inspect her arm.

And then something gripped her ankle and began to pull. What little air Ness had held in her body bubbled to the surface as she let out a silent scream in the blackness of the water. Something was dragging her down. A hand with fingers of icy iron.

All wish for knowledge, but none wish to pay the cost.

Traditional proverb

CHAPTER TWENTY-FIVE
DEATH DREAM

Ness floated in blackness. Water filled her mouth and throat. She felt its coldness in her lungs but somehow she wasn't drowning. She didn't even feel a sense of panic. Beneath her a dim light glowed. She stared down, drifting towards it, pulled as if by a current. The light grew stronger and Ness watched as a scene flickered into view.

She recognised the nursery straight away; her bed with its flowered bedspread, a fire crackling merrily behind the guard, dolls and toy soldiers scattered across the thick rug. Ness could only see the back of the little girl's head as she sat on her mother's knee, her black hair tied in rags, but Ness knew she looked on her own younger self. Her mother's long blonde hair spilled down her shoulder and over Ness's. Ness could smell her perfume. They wore their nightgowns and shadows danced on the walls to the wavering of a candle flame. Her mother held a book open and read to Ness.

'*After the merchant had eaten,*' her mother read, '*since he was a devout Mussulman, he washed and knelt to pray. Just then a terrible djinn, all red with rage, appeared, holding a cruel scimitar.*

'*"Stand up, merchant," cried the djinn. "Stand up that I may kill you, because you have murdered my only child."*

'*The merchant was terrified and protested his innocence. "How could I have murdered your child?"*

'*"How?" the furious djinn roared. "Did you not just now throw one of your date stones away without even a thought?"*

'*"I did," the merchant said, fearing for his life. "But, kind djinn, I meant no harm!"*

'*"No harm?" exclaimed the djinn. "My son was walking past and the stone struck him in the eye, killing him in an instant. Therefore you must die!" So saying, the djinn flung the merchant to the ground and raised the scimitar to cut off his head.*'

'Did the djinn love his son very much?' the little Ness asked her mother, her voice echoing through Ness's own lips.

'As much as life itself,' her mother said, burying her face in Ness's hair. 'As much as I love you, my only wish, my dear Necessity.'

Tears stung Ness's eyes as the young Ness pulled away from her mother and lifted her face upward. 'Would Papa kill the merchant if he'd killed me?'

But Ness didn't hear the answer. She could only stare at her own infant image. The little girl's eyes burned with a blue flame; they had no pupils, irises or even eyeballs, just two burning chasms. There was no candle, in fact; the shadows danced to the light of the child Necessity's eyes.

The waters of the pool swirled and shifted. Ness found herself in the scene, wrapped in her mother's arms, as she screamed. A dark shadow loomed over them and Ness saw the scabbed and peeling face of Zaakiel closing in on her. The blue light from her eyes seemed to sharpen every detail. Scaly fingers closed around her throat and Ness clawed at the face, gouging at the stitched eyes. Bile rose in her throat as the djinn blinked his crusted eyelids open and Ness found herself dazzled by a burning flame as blue as the light of her own eyes.

The nursery vanished now and the coldness of the water seeped into her bones. She pushed away from the djinn, kicking at the hand that gripped her ankle. Glancing down, she could see dim, human shapes reaching up from the fronds of weed that swayed at the murky bottom of the pool.

Something hooked an arm under her shoulder and she felt herself being dragged towards the surface. Ness gripped the arm and kicked again at whatever clawed at her leg.

The heat of the oasis hit her as she broke the surface. Grinning, Azuli heaved her on to the bank. Suddenly the water in her body became real once more and, giving a choking gasp, Ness vomited black liquid on to the mossy ground beneath her.

The water boiled behind her and she heard Azuli hiss a curse as he dragged her further back from the edge. Ness turned to see pale hands grasping upward from the pool, splashing the water and clawing the muddy bank as they reached for her in vain.

'Azuli!' Ness panted, hugging him. 'You're safe, you're . . . How? I thought . . .' She stopped and ran her hand over her once-broken arm. 'My arm,' she murmured. She felt strong, revitalized. 'That has to be the Pool of Life.'

'And you had to go and fall in it,' Azuli said.

'I'm so glad you're safe!' Ness hugged him again. 'Tell me what happened!'

Azuli gave a grin, wincing from a split in his lip and the hug. His face was filthy and a purple bruise blossomed on his temple. His grin faded and he looked pale and serious.

'The carpet threw me off. I was lucky – a web of creepers broke my fall and left me dangling like a worm on a hook. It took me half the night to cut myself down without breaking my neck! But I think if I'd got down sooner I wouldn't be here now. I saw some horrible things crawling along the jungle floor below me.' Azuli cast his eyes to the ground for a second.

'I can imagine,' Ness whispered, thinking of Grubb and the camp.

They sat in the clearing in silence for a moment. The pool filled the centre of the glade, which was walled in by the thick blackness of the oasis. Thick, dark, glossy-leaved plants fringed the water. A few reeds sprouted between them. The pool looked unremarkable and yet there was something faintly disgusting about its black water and the surrounding plants.

'I was trying to find the edge of the oasis when I heard you crashing through the trees. So I came looking for you – just in time to see you fall in! What was down there?'

'It was horrible.' Ness shuddered. 'Like a dream. Mama was reading me a story from *The Arabian Nights* and then the djinn came. His eyes, they were blue fire . . . but so were mine . . .'

Ness told him every detail that she could remember; of the vision in the pool; she told him about Grubb, the bloodsuckers, how she'd shattered her arm and ribs and yet they were healed and stronger than ever.

'It doesn't make sense.' Azuli frowned, shook his head. 'Scrabsnitch said that the pool gives the answers a seeker needs. Do you think you had some kind of answer?'

Ness shook her head. 'It's a very confusing one if it is an answer.'

'Well,' Azuli said, standing up and striding towards the pool, 'there are two of us so we have two chances. Maybe I can get some answers.'

'Azuli, no!' Ness cried. 'There are things down there. Horrible, half-decayed things.'

'Can they be any worse than the djinn or the Pestilents?' Azuli said, glancing back at Ness.

As if in answer to his question, the water began to boil. A filthy brown scum fizzed on the surface, a stench of rotten vegetation and earth filled the clearing around the pool.

Slowly a huge figure rose from the centre of the pool. Ten times the size of Ness or Azuli, it towered over them, waist deep in the seething waters. It looked human in shape but a composite of many crushed and distorted corpses. The torso was made up of bodies, decayed and twisted together. Limb after twisted, broken limb wrapped and tangled one around another to form its arms. Its head too was composed of many human heads crushed together like so much clay or mud. Ness could see eyes blinking from its cheeks, mouths opening and closing like drowning fish. The skin melted back into the waters, dripping brown and green.

'Who disturbs the Sleepers of the Amarant?' the creature said, its voice wet and rattling.

'My name,' Azuli croaked, stumbling backward from the pool's edge, 'is Azuli, son of the Lashkars of Sulayman. Who . . . who are you?'

The creature tilted its hideous head slightly as if thinking. Four eyes blinked in its forehead and then vanished under a tide of molten flesh. 'We are those who came here seeking the Amarant and never left,' the Sleepers said. Ness stared at the bodies writhing in its huge form. 'Tortured souls snared by the siren glow of the Flower of Life.'

'Can you help us?' Ness called, choking on the stink from the pool, disgusted to think she had just fallen into that water, inhaled it. 'I need to find my parents.'

'The Pool of Life has healed you, Necessity Bonehill,' the Sleepers gargled. 'It has shown you something of what you need to know. Your parents are held by the djinn Zaakiel.'

'Then tell *me* more,' Azuli demanded, taking a step forward.

'Once, we could see all lives, all futures. We knew everything that had been and would be,' the Sleepers wailed. 'The Amarant burned bright in the Pool of Life and we guarded it jealously.'

'But someone took the Amarant,' Ness murmured. 'And you were left here with no purpose?'

'The Amarant is no more,' the creature said, and Ness thought a sob caught its voice. 'Stolen by the greedy. Only the merest traces of it exist. Our power wanes. We cannot see clearly.'

'Nevertheless,' Azuli said, 'I would know how to find the djinn Zaakiel and destroy him.'

'On the highest house on the highest hill,' the Sleepers whispered, melting back into the pool. 'There Zaakiel views his destruction and revels in it. You will know how to destroy him.' It swept a dripping hand across the ground in front of them. 'But remember: sometimes the simplest story holds a seed of wisdom in its heart.'

A sword glinted silver in the moss. Next to it lay a golden cross and beside that a wooden platter piled with dates.

'Take sustenance, then choose your weapons carefully.'

With a final sigh, the Sleepers of the Amarant slipped back into the Pool of Life.

Azuli leapt forward and snatched up the silver sword,

giving it a few test swings. 'It's beautiful,' he whispered. 'Maybe with this we'll have a chance.'

'I'm not sure.' Ness shook her head. 'Besides, it doesn't have Zaakiel's name carved in the blade.'

'We could carve it.' Azuli's eyes burned with excitement. 'Remember how Morris's bullets hurt the djinn?'

'They didn't kill him outright though,' Ness mused, stroking a finger over the cross. She picked a date from the platter and popped it into her mouth. 'What about this cross?'

'What, are you going to hit Zaakiel with the cross?' Azuli snorted, taking a fruit too and chewing it. 'No, the sword is the weapon.'

'I wonder,' Ness said, picking up another date. 'You take the sword then.'

Azuli whirled the blade, but stopped, suddenly deflated. 'Not that it matters.'

Ness frowned. 'What do you mean?'

Azuli threw his hands in the air. 'We're trapped here – the carpet is gone. How are we going to get back?'

A loyal friend is worth more than gold.

Traditional proverb

CHAPTER TWENTY-SIX
ESCAPE FROM THE JUNGLE

Azuli threw his hands to his sides. 'It's useless,' he muttered. 'We are thousands of miles from London.'

'Then we have no choice. We've got to find that carpet,' Ness said, squinting up into the canopy of the oasis and chewing on another date.

'It'll be long gone by now,' Azuli murmured, following her gaze.

'I think not.' Ness beamed, pointing above her head.

High up, the carpet hung limp. A branch pierced its middle, trapping it. Briars and creepers snagged and tangled themselves around it.

'It must have got stuck up there when it crashed through the trees and threw you off,' Azuli said, running to the bottom of a wide trunk and peering up. 'I'll climb up and free it.'

'*We'll* climb up,' Ness said, spitting out and pocketing the date stones. She joined him and grasped a low branch.

The tree bark cooled Ness's hands as she climbed. It felt smooth, slippery at times, but there were enough branches radiating out from the central trunk to make climbing easy. Azuli's panting echoed with hers across the jungle as they went higher and higher.

Ness's mind wandered with the monotony of the climb. *Why didn't the bloodsuckers kill me? Did the djinn mark me as his own in some way? And what about London? Will we get back in time and what will we find if we do?*

'Er, Ness,' Azuli said, looking down – but beyond her, to the ground below.

Ness turned and stared down. Pale faces glared back at them, shrouded partly by the foliage of the trees, but Ness caught a glimpse of khaki and a flash of sharp white teeth.

'Bloodsuckers?' Azuli croaked, watching as two of the soldiers began clambering up the tree towards them.

'Climb up, Azuli, quickly,' Ness hissed. 'Fast as you can. They aren't after me – I don't know why – but they'll want you. Get that carpet free then I'll hold them off.'

Azuli scrambled towards the flapping carpet like a frightened squirrel, slipping every now and then.

'Give us the boy,' the captain called up. His voice still had the clipped tone of an officer but something cold lurked under the surface sound. 'You can go free, girl. We cannot feast on you.'

'Why not?' Ness spat. 'Not good enough?'

'Give us the boy,' the captain snapped.

'Go to hell!' Ness snarled back.

The captain allowed a smirk to twist his pointed features, then he barked an order in a language Ness didn't understand. The bloodsuckers moved steadily, purposefully. Ness climbed more slowly, allowing Azuli to gain height.

The first soldier reached out for her ankle. Ness pulled her foot up and then slammed it back, her heel catching the creature in the eye. With a roar, the bloodsucker put his hand up to his face and Ness, sensing his loss of balance, gave him another kick to the shoulder.

The soldier jerked back, waving his arms in the air as he sought stability. But his weight had shifted too far off the branch and Ness watched with satisfaction as he fell, bones cracking as he bounced from branch to branch and finally landed on the ground with a thump, forcing the captain to take a step back.

'I'm nearly there,' Azuli called.

The branches were thinner near the top, bending and cracking under their weight. The carpet began twisting and pulling at the briars that snagged it, like a wild animal in a trap, but the sharp branch was punched through its middle like a meat hook, holding it tight. Azuli stretched to reach the far corner of the carpet.

Something gripped Ness's ankle and she glanced down to see the second bloodsucker's triumphant grin. Ness tried to kick but the creature's grip held. With a gasp, she hooked her arms over the branch above her, desperate not to be dragged off and thrown to the ground so far below. She tried to lash out but he had her legs pinned.

Slowly, the weight on her legs increased as the bloodsucker bore down. Her shoulders burning with the effort, Ness wriggled to keep hold of the branch.

'You'll not drag me down,' she hissed, staring at the leering creature.

A shaft of warm sunlight lanced down from above as Azuli struggled through the canopy. The bloodsucker gave a hideous scream and Ness screwed her eyes up, glimpsing the seared flesh of his face in the light. She couldn't block out the stink of burning flesh. The soldier's grasp relaxed and Ness risked a look as he fell to his doom, trailing stinking smoke.

'It's the daylight!' Ness called up. 'Grubb said something about them not being able to live in the sunlight.'

But more bloodsuckers were scrambling up the tree. Ness climbed higher to where Azuli tugged at the edge of the rippling carpet.

'I can't get it free!' he groaned.

'Never mind that,' she said. 'Help me pull these branches apart.'

The soldiers came closer, eyes fixed on Azuli, clambering branch over branch with ruthless efficiency.

Ness tore and snapped at thin branches, becoming reckless and swinging on some of the thicker limbs until they creaked. Azuli hacked at the canopy with his silver blade.

The captain shouted commands from below and the creatures increased their climbing pace.

'Faster, Azuli,' Ness panted, ripping at the leaves above

them. Azuli gave a mirthless grin and swung his blade harder, sending branches and stems fluttering to the floor below.

Gradually, a hole appeared in the treetops and the fierce light of the desert replaced the cool shadows. Screams sounded beneath them and Ness glanced down to see more blackened skin and smouldering corpses falling on to their comrades. A pang of pity stabbed through her. These were men once, with families; they didn't ask to be changed. It was the oasis that bred this evil. She wished she could burn the whole thing down.

The captain stared up from the dank ground, malice burning in his eyes. He shook his fist and then vanished into the darkness of the jungle.

'We did it.' Ness grinned at Azuli, leaning over to hug him, then wobbling to regain her balance.

'Ness, look out!' Azuli yelled.

Ness spun round to see the carpet working itself free from the branch. A huge rent hung in its centre; the carpet had been hurling itself back and forth to widen the hole. Now only a few strands held it.

Ignoring the dizzying drop below, Ness threw herself at the carpet, grabbing the corner as it launched free.

'Here we go again!' she said through gritted teeth.

Azuli leapt on to it too and hooked his arm through the hole, grinning fiercely.

The carpet whisked upward and Ness dragged herself to the front.

'Now listen,' Ness bellowed at it. 'You can't win. I won't let you. Just behave and take us back to London.'

Ness's stomach seemed to force its way into her throat as the carpet gave a few rebellious dips, dives and somersaults, but then it flattened out and began to accelerate skyward.

A cool breeze fanned Ness and Azuli as they watched the oasis shrink through the hole in the middle of the carpet.

The day dragged by and, despite the carpet's incredible speed, the landscape below remained stubbornly brown and arid.

'What if it's taking us in the wrong direction, just out of spite?' Azuli whispered at one point.

Ness shook her head. 'It wouldn't dare. We travelled for a long time to get here. We just have to be patient.'

Easier said than done, Ness thought. *What on earth awaits us in London?*

The air gradually grew cooler then bitterly cold. Cloud obscured their view of the land below and it seemed to Ness that they flew in another world, comprised of mist and fog.

The journey rolled on. Ness and Azuli huddled together for warmth – as best they could with a huge gaping hole between them.

'Do you think we can stop the djinn?' Azuli muttered after long hours of silence.

'I don't know,' she replied, feeling the date stones in her pocket. 'But we have to try.'

'What do you think your vision in the pool meant?' Azuli said, frowning.

'I don't know exactly,' Ness murmured. 'What I wanted was a way to destroy Zaakiel.'

'The blade will do that,' Azuli said, smoothing his palm along the flat edge of his scimitar.

'No. Remember what Hafid said about brains winning this battle, not brawn?' Ness replied. 'If nothing else, I've learned my lesson.'

'What do you mean?' Azuli said.

'I used to think that only the strong survive,' Ness sighed. 'My father drummed that into me. Every man for himself and the devil take the hindmost.'

'But you don't think that now?' Azuli said, narrowing his eyes at her.

'I'd give anything to go back and save the girls at the Academy,' Ness said, choking back a sob, 'and all those poor people who worked for Lumm and the others who have become Pestilents.'

'But we can't change the past. I can't change the fact that I lost the sword. We can't bring *people* back from the dead,' Azuli said, looking grim. 'Widow Quilfy tried that, didn't she?'

Ness shuddered. So much had happened in such a short time. They sat silently and watched the light fading from their world of cloud.

'I know but I was such a . . . a bully,' Ness said, sniffing.

'If there's any way I can make it all right then I'll take that chance.'

'And I'll help you.' Azuli smiled and stroked away her tears with the back of his hand.

'Tomorrow is day seven,' Ness whispered to herself. 'Tomorrow Zaakiel grants my wish, but it'll cost me everything.'

A GOOD ANVIL DOES NOT FEAR THE HAMMER.

TRADITIONAL PROVERB

CHAPTER TWENTY-SEVEN

THE SEVENTH DAY

Dawn crept over the horizon, revealing the distant domes and spires of London to Ness and Azuli. The city grew, a stain spreading across the landscape, and the smell of smoke filled Ness's nostrils. She drew a long, deep breath.

'I never thought I'd find the stink of London welcome,' she grinned, blotting out the thoughts of what lurked down there and what they would soon face.

'Shall we go to Scrabsnitch's or to Arabesque Alley?' Azuli said, returning her grin with a tight smile.

'The Alley,' Ness said, her voice wavering. 'We need to find out if Hafid has located the djinn and your father will be worried. Besides, I don't think I could bear it if we went to the emporium and found . . .'

Azuli gave a brief nod and squeezed her hand.

The river became an ever-thickening ribbon until they could see the ships cutting through the black waters.

'Is it just the view from up here or are there fewer boats on the river?' Azuli said, frowning.

'And they're all heading east,' Ness added. 'Away from the city.'

'The djinn's evil must have spread,' Azuli gasped, pointing down.

The streets seethed with people running in every direction. Horses whinnied, rearing as people crushed past them. Ness could pick out overturned barrows, their contents of fruit or fish scattered across the cobbles. Here and there preachers ranted at small groups of kneeling onlookers. Their angry cries mingled with the yells and calls of the panicked crowds and the occasional muffled explosion. Ness could see plumes of smoke rising all over the horizon.

The thin, green mist drifted across the city but was still thickest around the tight knot of dilapidated houses and twisting narrow streets that surrounded Arabesque Alley. The carpet flew down, skimming the heads of the terrified crowd. The fog grew more dense and the streets became emptier and more desolate.

'Where have all the Pestilents gone?' Ness frowned. 'There should be an army of them filling these alleyways.'

Gradually they came to the alcove and Azuli gave a gasp. The blue gate hung on one hinge, splintered and dangling inwards. Ness yanked the carpet up, red brick and grey roof slate flashed past them, and her stomach lurched as she forced the carpet down into the alley on the other side of the gate.

'Oh no,' Ness gasped.

The Alley lay littered with Pestilents. Here and there were huddled shapes, those Lashkars who had made a valiant last stand against the tide of evil. In the distance Ness could hear the tumult of the city, but a deathly hush hung over the Alley. Somewhere water trickled from a bullet-holed barrel.

'Are we too late?' Azuli muttered, his knuckles whitening around the scimitar's handle.

Ness said nothing but sent the carpet skimming over the destruction towards Hafid's quarters. The Pestilents had obviously squeezed into this narrow alley, almost unable to move. They lay piled on top of each other, filling the passage, crushed against the doors.

'There was a fierce battle here,' Ness said, gripping Azuli's hand. 'We'll have to go in through an upper window.'

Ness guided the carpet to one of the windows and peered in. A rifle barrel poked cold against her nose. Behind it, confusion creased Scrabsnitch's face, followed by wide-eyed recognition.

'Azuli! Miss Bonehill!' he cried. 'We thought you were gone, never to return.'

'Mr Scrabsnitch,' Ness replied, equally confused. 'But what are you doing here? I mean –'

'Let us get in, Ness,' Azuli said, giving a tight smile. 'Or are we going to chat like this all day?'

'Do forgive me,' Scrabsnitch stammered, jumping back.

Ness guided the carpet through the narrow window. She squinted in the gloom. Refugees from other houses lined the chamber. Old Lashkar men and women, coughing, sobbing.

Scrabsnitch shook his head. 'The Pestilents started moving a few hours ago. They were slow and clumsy but there were so many of them.'

'Where's my father? Jabalah? Hafid?' Azuli asked urgently, grabbing Scrabsnitch's sleeve.

Scrabsnitch shook his head and sighed. 'They fought their way out of Arabesque Alley but I was left here to guard Hafid.'

'Can you get me some rope or a belt?' Ness grunted, kneeling on the protesting carpet and rolling it up inch by inch.

'Er, yes.' Scrabsnitch glanced around, then pulled a length of rope from his pocket and handed it over, grinning. 'Here we are. Lucky I picked that up before.'

The grin quickly faded as he led them down through the building. Worried faces peered from every shadow in the house. Old and tired, the last of the Lashkars of Sulayman crowded and huddled in every room they passed. Some sat on the stairways. Others lay on pallets, groaning from infected wounds.

Hafid sat, cross-legged and alone, in the centre of the room where Ness had first met him. His eyes were squeezed shut and he muttered and mumbled under his breath.

'He's casting a charm over the remaining Lashkars and Sergeant Major Morris,' Scrabsnitch whispered.

'Morris is alive?' Ness said. 'How did you escape from the djinn?'

'Another piece of incredible luck.' Scrabsnitch gave a thin, self-satisfied smile. 'The emporium collapsed in on us.'

'That's luck?' Azuli murmured.

'Well,' Scrabsnitch said, smoothing his wispy beard. 'I managed to drag Morris behind a solid granite statue of Moloch. To cut a long story short, the whole shop collapsed and, by some stroke of luck, the djinn couldn't find us or assumed we were dead. He just left.' Scrabsnitch gave a snort of delight, then covered his mouth. 'So once we'd dug ourselves out, we came here to see if there was any news of you.'

'What did you . . . find?' Hafid croaked, half turning his head.

Ness hurried over to the feeble figure. 'Riddles and dreams,' she muttered.

'I'm sorry I can't . . . be of . . . more help,' Hafid gasped, his breathing heavy. 'I am . . . struggling to keep the . . . contagion from the last fighting party.'

'I had a vision. My mother read me a story,' Ness said, reluctant to relive the experience. 'I had eyes of blue fire. When the djinn grabbed me, our eyes were the same.'

'Which story?' Hafid hissed. Sweat trickled down his wrinkled brow.

'*The Merchant and the Djinn*,' Ness said, frowning, 'from the *Arabian Nights* book I used to have . . . But they're just children's tales.'

'Ha!' Hafid's whole body shook with silent laughter. 'Ancient tales . . . told around the campfires of many in the old countries . . . We seek our wisdom in our holy books these days but these stories . . . were told for a reason. Think about the tale. You have your answer there.'

My answer to killing the djinn? Ness thought. *But it doesn't find my parents.*

Hafid took a breath and retreated into his deep concentration.

'My father and the others, where did they go?' Azuli asked, grabbing Scrabsnitch by the shoulders.

'Hafid has tracked Zaakiel to St Paul's Cathedral,' Scrabsnitch said, shaking his head. 'He suspects that the fiend wants the best vantage point from which to view the carnage.'

'The highest house,' Azuli whispered. 'That's what the guardian of the oasis said . . . On the highest hill.'

There Zaakiel views his destruction and revels in it, Ness thought. *That's where my parents will be.*

'The cathedral is on Ludgate Hill, the highest hill in London,' Scrabsnitch added. 'Your father and the remaining Lashkars were not content to wait here. They fought their way out and are heading for St Paul's.'

'Then we must find them and join them,' Azuli declared, turning to leave.

'No,' Ness said, grabbing his shoulder. 'Our job is to battle the djinn.'

'But the Lashkars will surely die,' Azuli cried, yanking his shoulder from Ness's hand.

'And we will die with them if we try to help,' Ness said, her voice calm. 'But if we kill the djinn before they reach him, we can save them and everyone else. My parents, your father, everyone. And I think I know how to do it.'

The tyrant is only the slave turned inside out.

Traditional proverb

CHAPTER TWENTY-EIGHT
COUNTER-ATTACK

Scrabsnitch waved them off as they unfurled the carpet, leapt on and flew out of the window, heading towards the distant crouching dome of St Paul's.

'And how do you propose to defeat Zaakiel?' Azuli wondered aloud.

'Think about the *Arabian Nights* tale,' Ness said. 'The djinn's son, how is he killed?'

'The merchant casts a date stone away and it strikes the djinn's son . . . in the eye.' Azuli's speech slowed as realisation dawned on him. 'That is madness! You think you can kill the djinn with a date stone?'

'Hafid told me to think about the story,' Ness said. 'He said there was a reason that people told the tales. They're ancient wisdom.'

'But the Sleepers of the Amarant gave us this,' Azuli said, patting the hilt of the silver sword. He had made a point of scratching Zaakiel's name on the blade with a dagger point before they left.

Ness looked dubiously at the sword. 'They said to take sustenance and to choose our weapons carefully,' she replied, pulling a handful of date stones from her pocket. 'I think they meant these.'

'And how are you going to get close enough to throw them with sufficient force to kill?' Azuli said, looking incredulous.

Ness avoided Azuli's steady gaze.

Even in the short time they'd been back, Ness could sense that things had worsened in the city. Screams echoed up from the streets, more plumes of smoke rose above the roofline where fires had started. As they flew, she could see crowds of people trying to evade the streams of Pestilents that lurched along, spreading poison through the streets. They grabbed at the terrified survivors, gouging and strangling, their decaying faces twisted in a mindless rage. Ness squeezed her eyes shut and let the cool air blast her face. *The djinn must be stopped.*

'There!' Azuli shouted, pointing downward.

Ness peered over the edge of the carpet. The Lashkars stood back to back at the junction of several roads, surrounded by an ever-increasing mass of Pestilents. The weak sun flashed on their scimitar blades and every now and then a small puff of gun smoke drifted up from the crowd, followed by the throaty roar of Morris's blunderbuss.

'We must help them!' Azuli pleaded.

'No.' Ness stared ahead through the haze of smoke at the bulk of the cathedral.

'We must save your father and leave mine to die?' Azuli snarled. 'Is that it?'

Ness shook her head. Tears stung her eyes. 'Our parents don't matter now, Azuli,' she sobbed. 'Only stopping the djinn and saving mankind from this hideous plague matters.'

'Then at least let's buy them some time,' Azuli begged, his eyes glittering. 'With the carpet we can cut through whole swathes of those accursed creatures!'

Ness stared into Azuli's pleading brown eyes and then heaved a sigh. 'I'll try to steer it down but we can't waste any time,' she muttered. 'And I can't guarantee the carpet will behave itself.'

'I wish you could control it completely,' Azuli sighed as Ness forced the carpet downward.

For a moment the world flashed blue, forcing Ness to blink and shake her head. She looked up to see Azuli staring at her.

'What now?' she snapped irritably.

But before he could answer, the carpet went slack as if all the life had drained from it. Ness felt her stomach turn as they lost height.

'What's all this?' she growled. 'Fly, damn you! Take these Pestilent creatures off their feet!'

As if Ness's words had breathed new life into it, the carpet swirled around, almost unseating them. It plunged down towards the seething mass of bodies. Ness gripped the rough weave, gagging on the stench that blew up from the creatures. Azuli yelled, slashing left and right with his sword as the carpet bowled into Pestilent after Pestilent, sending them crashing to the ground. For a moment Ness forgot everything else – her parents, Azuli, the Lashkars. She was one with the carpet. It was one with her and followed her every command.

The roar of Morris's gun grew nearer and the startled face of Taimur flashed past them. The carpet took them in a dizzying circuit of the tight-knit group. Jabalah let out a cheer as the Pestilents staggered back from them, creating space. Morris gave a grin and saluted Ness. She returned his grin and then pulled them back up into the air and looked down.

But as she waved her heart plummeted. More Pestilents swarmed in from the side streets, others staggered from houses to replace those that had fallen.

'We have to stop the djinn,' Ness bellowed.

Azuli nodded, his face ashen.

The carpet whipped them through the sooty air towards the dome of St Paul's. It loomed over the city, black and squat, making Ness think of some kind of beetle rather than a place of worship.

'There, on the lantern,' Azuli snapped, pointing to the tower that jutted up from the great dome. 'Up on the golden cross.'

'Mama, Father,' Ness gasped. Her heart pounded.

Clinging, frozen, to the main upright of the golden cross that topped the cathedral stood Eliza and Anthony

Bonehill. Zaakiel crouched on the left arm of the cross, cackling at the carnage that unfolded below.

Ness could see her mother's fine features stained by tears, her blonde hair blown by the breeze. Beside her, Father's dark face was calm and stern. No matter how uncaring they'd been, they were still her parents.

'We can save them,' cried Azuli.

'No,' Ness murmured, her throat dry. 'It's the djinn we need to catch. Get me in close,' she hissed at the carpet. 'Quickly, before he notices us.'

Ness dragged the carpet round and leaned forward so that its speed increased. Zaakiel stared up, consternation flickering across his face to be replaced with an evil grin. He jumped up, standing on the cross and swinging out to offer Ness the fullest target.

The carpet swept in. Ness felt she could almost touch Zaakiel. He wore some kind of robe that billowed in the wind. She could see the open sores where Morris had blasted him in the emporium. Ness pulled the stones from her pocket and readied herself to launch them at the festering creature.

'It won't work, Ness,' Azuli cried. 'His eyes – they're stitched shut! The stones can't hurt him!'

But Ness had already committed herself to the throw. She watched as the date stones passed straight through Zaakiel's smoky form and rattled uselessly against the cross.

Ness steered the carpet down to the roof below the dome. She felt numb.

'I've failed,' she whispered.

'We still have the sword,' Azuli growled.

They turned to face the djinn as he floated down from the dome, his robes billowing in a pestilent breeze.

'It is day seven, Necessity,' Zaakiel hissed. 'It's time to grant your wish!'

I wish, I wish, but it's all in vain,
I wish I was a maid again.

'Died for Love', traditional folk ballad

CHAPTER TWENTY-NINE

THE DEATH WISH

Zaakiel stood on the roof before them, a mocking grin stretching his pock-marked skull of a face.

'Is that why you did that?' Ness hissed through gritted teeth. 'Stitched your eyelids, as protection?'

'Yes.' The djinn scowled. 'But not against clumsily thrown date stones.

'The second person to free me from the bottle was a woman. She wore rich silks and a golden crown. *This one has no need of gold*, I thought. *Maybe she will make a gracious wish.*

'"My husband's mother is an interfering old witch," the queen said. "For my first wish, I would have you turn her into the lowliest worm. For my second, I would have you send an ugly crow to devour her. And for my third, I would have you return to your bottle."

'I tried not to watch the queen's mother-in-law as she melted into another form only to be consumed by the ugliest of birds. I couldn't bear to see the terrible things men made me do, so I tried to claw my eyes out. When that didn't work, I stitched them shut.

'But three thousand years ground on. Every single man, woman and child who opened the bottle displayed themselves at their worst. A creature of pure magic cannot help but see, hear and feel every scream, cry and whimper. And every disgusting demand.

'Make my sister ugly. Give me my neighbour's house and farm. Kill my son. Burn that city to the ground. Give me more gold than I can ever carry home. Drown those children.

'My words were twisted, extra wishes were tricked out of me. Every sin, every vice, every excess was indulged until I could bear it no longer. And I couldn't even take comfort in the fact that for many of the wishers it ended badly, because too many of them profited from their perverse wishes while the innocent suffered.

'*The next person who opens this bottle will have one wish and then I will kill them and be free*, I thought to myself. *Then I shall rid the blue-green earth of this infestation called mankind once and for all with a plague the likes of which have never been seen.*'

'Just stop.' Ness spat. 'Why do you insist on telling me these stories?'

'They are more than stories, Necessity. We cannot control the magic that flows in our veins,' Zaakiel groaned. 'You could not imagine the depths of man's depravity; his cruelty has no limits. Your father, even –'

'My father?' Ness echoed, glancing upward to the distant figures shivering at the base of the golden cross.

'Do you think your father wished for a wealthy inheritance without knowing full well that your grandparents would die?' Zaakiel grinned, his needle teeth yellow against dark green gums. 'And he has plans for you and I both.'

'Let them go,' Ness growled. Her mind felt numb. She was tired of riddles and puzzles and wishes.

'He murdered Carlos Grossford knowing it would bring all of this,' the djinn said, waving an open hand at the carnage below. 'He is a devious and evil man. That's why I put him up there. Even Anthony Bonehill can't fly, and while he stands up there he can watch the destruction he has brought upon mankind through his greed and selfishness.'

'Enough!' Azuli snarled, slashing at the djinn with the scimitar. 'I tire of all this talking. You are evil, Zaakiel, and you shall pay for your crimes.'

'You see, you can't trust them,' Zaakiel said, stumbling back, a wicked grin darkening his twisted face. 'This boy never gives up, does he?'

'Azuli, don't!' Ness yelled.

'Oh, it seems the young lady cares about you, young man,' the djinn cackled, sidestepping another swing.

Azuli grunted as he hacked down with the blade once more, forcing the djinn back along the roof.

'Do you think that blade is going to stop me simply because you scratched my name on it with a rusty nail, boy?' The djinn clicked his fingers and Azuli froze, staring into space.

'Zaakiel, stop!' Ness cried, stepping forward. 'Don't hurt him. Why can't you just go? You can be free at last. Leave mankind alone and just go!'

'You think mankind would leave me in peace? No, men are ruled by greed. But you are different, Necessity Bonehill,' Zaakiel hissed from behind her. 'You are not like them, can't you feel it? The boy knows. He could tell you, if I let him.'

'Why do you torment us so?' Ness hugged Azuli closer.

'It is nothing compared to the torment you will endure if you don't join me,' Zaakiel said, circling around them, prising the sword from Azuli's rigid grip.

'Join you?' Ness said. 'What do you mean? Why would I join you?'

'Tell her, Azuli.' Zaakiel grinned at Ness over Azuli's shoulder. 'Tell her what you know.'

Azuli collapsed into Ness's arms as the djinn released him. 'I wish you had a date stone in your mouth,' Azuli whispered in her ear and gave Ness a sad smile. She frowned in confusion.

'Watch this.' Zaakiel rammed the sword through Azuli's back. Ness gave a scream as the point of the huge butcher's blade cut through Azuli and into her stomach.

But Ness felt nothing. Releasing Azuli, she stared down at her unharmed torso. Ness stumbled, watching as Zaakiel wrenched the sword back, leaving Azuli swaying for a second before crumpling into a heap. Blood pooled at Ness's feet. Azuli's blood.

'Hmm,' Zaakiel smirked. 'They're better for hacking, these swords, but this one's very sharp. A shame, he was such a brave little boy.'

A cold numbness swept over Ness. *This isn't happening.*

The djinn stamped forward, still gripping Azuli's scimitar. 'Why didn't the sword harm you, Necessity?' he murmured.

Ness shook her head.

'Why must you join me, Necessity?'

Ness couldn't answer.

'Because you are a djinn like me,' Zaakiel bellowed. 'A creature born of a wish. Created by magic. My magic.'

That's why the bloodsuckers rejected me. They wanted human blood. I'm not human.

A huge date stone filled Ness's mouth. *Azuli's last wish. He knew.*

'You wished that your parents loved you,' Zaakiel hissed, bringing his face close to hers. 'But nothing is so simple. Your mother's heartfelt, fervent wish was for you. A pure wish for once, but the world had tainted my heart by then. That's all she ever wanted. You.' Zaakiel dropped Azuli's sword and grabbed Ness's shoulders. 'I could have made you the spawn of Anthony Bonehill. Instead I made you a djinni child, a creature of pure magic. Bonehill loves your power. He hunted down the bloodstone so he could bind you, not me.'

Ness broke his gaze, stared down at Azuli's shattered body. He'd been so beautiful. Her first friend. Her first love.

'You know your true nature,' Zaakiel hissed. 'How else did you cure Azuli? How did you escape from him when you first went to search for Lumm? How did you control the carpet so easily all of a sudden? You granted wishes. Your power is raw, untrained, granting unlimited wishes even without your knowledge. But now you are of an age when your magic shows itself to the world. Your eyes burn blue like mine. Join me. Mankind will die. We will live.'

My eyes burn blue? Ness grazed her fingers over her eyes and felt a cold tingling. Azuli had seen her change; Morris and the Lashkars too. That's why they had stared at her. Fury boiled in Ness's gut as she realised what the djinn was asking her to do.

She lashed out, a slap that turned Zaakiel's head, then she fell on him, her sharp nails pinching at the hard crusted threads that puckered the skin of his eyelids. Ness's scream of rage drowned Zaakiel's scream of pain as she felt the thin flesh pop and rip to reveal blue flame.

Ness gripped Zaakiel's head and spat the stone deep into his blazing left eye. With a roar of pain, the djinn swung away, sending Ness spinning towards the edge of the roof.

'What have you done?' he gasped, holding his hand to his face. 'We could have been happy. The last djinns in our own Garden of Eden.'

Ness felt the roof slip from beneath her feet but slapped her palms on to the balustrade, stopping her fall. She hung helplessly, her shoulders burning, as Zaakiel staggered towards her.

'Your wish has come true,' he wept, shaking and trembling. His skin began to pulse and boil. 'Your father and mother both love you, but you should find out exactly what it is about you that they love.'

He gave a rasping, bitter laugh which turned to a yell of horror as a woody tendril popped from his neck and wrapped around his shoulder. More roots burst forth. Zaakiel screamed and shook as his maimed arm split open to reveal a gnarled branch. Then, with a final howl of agony, a huge trunk of a date palm exploded from within the djinn's body.

Sobbing, Ness swung her leg up on to the balustrade and heaved herself up on to the roof, oblivious to the pooling pus and gore. For a moment she lay still. Chaos continued to sound all over the city. Ness frowned and held her fingers up. They were turning into smoke.

Revenge is keener than an axe,
Love as soft as melting wax.

'Riddles Wisely Expounded', traditional folk ballad

CHAPTER THIRTY
A FATHER'S LOVE

Ness stared as her fingers grew transparent and insubstantial, drifting slightly in the breeze that blew across the rooftop of St Paul's Cathedral. Azuli lay still at her feet. She wanted to reach down and hug him but her body refused to move.

Her father's distant voice whispered in her ear, so familiar, and yet the words were strange, guttural, in a language she had never heard before.

Ness felt drowsy, light as a cloud. She drifted up towards the golden cross and her parents. Were they her parents? She was a djinn. She always had been different; now she knew why. Her mama loved her, had wished for her to be born. But her father?

That's where the voice is coming from, she thought. Her mind felt hazy as the words grew louder. *Father is calling to me*.

Anthony Bonehill perched at the base of the cross, one arm extended towards Ness. Her mother hung on with both hands, her eyes wide with fear.

Ness felt detached from the scene. The whole of London lay spread before her. Black smoke billowed across the skyline now and flames leapt high into the sky. Screams and howls echoed up from below, explosions and gunshots split the air. Crowds seethed along the streets, pursued by the slow but relentless Pestilents.

Ness drifted up until she floated opposite her father. The ring on his outstretched hands seemed huge, out of all proportion to the rest of him. The gem in the ring glowed red, warm and inviting.

'See, child, the bloodstone calls you,' said Bonehill. 'As it always has. I made sure of that.'

'Anthony, no!' Ness's mother screamed. 'You can't do this – she's our daughter!'

'Our daughter? This creature?' Bonehill's face twisted into a mask of derision. 'Look at her eyes, Eliza. They burn like a djinn's. But you knew that all along, didn't you?'

The red pulse from the ring seemed to call to Ness. *But Mama is upset*, she thought.

'I love her whatever she may be,' Eliza sobbed. 'She's my child. Don't force her into that ring, Anthony, please.'

'She must go in,' Bonehill said. 'This is what I have worked for, schemed and laboured for, all these years. You wished for the child, a stupid wish that forced Grossford to make his wish last because then *I* had to secure the family fortune.'

'Your wish for wealth took my parents from me.' Eliza's voice shook with rage and emotion. 'Now you want to take my daughter?'

'If you'd wished for wealth as we'd agreed, then you could have had a hundred children once I'd secured Zaakiel. But no, you messed things up,' Anthony snarled. 'In fact, it turned out better than I could have hoped. I knew that a child born of a pure wish would be a djinn. Imagine that! Having our own unspoiled djinn at our beck and call, not world-weary and cynical like Zaakiel. All I needed was a bloodstone.'

'But she has her own will and mind,' Eliza gasped, her eyes travelling across the smouldering skyline. 'And look at the cost – how many lives have been wasted? How many men, women and children killed?'

'We can sort all that out once Ness is under my power,' Bonehill murmured. 'She was safe at the Academy – everyone thought her dead.'

'You told everyone that I was dead?' Ness said, gazing at her mother's desperate face.

'I never wanted you to go, my darling,' Eliza sobbed. 'It broke my heart but I thought you'd be safer away from him and Carlos. I wanted to protect you.'

'But you never contacted me, never came to see me.'

'I knew I couldn't bear to see you only to be parted again,' Eliza sighed. 'I fooled myself that I was acting for the best. But I set Sergeant Major Morris to watch over you.'

'It would have been a simple case of waiting for her to come of age and inherit her powers but Carlos fouled things up,' Bonehill growled.

Ness listened with dazed curiosity as if she were watching a complex jigsaw puzzle being pieced together.

'But why did you kill him?' she asked, her voice seeming distant.

'You were near the age when your magic would manifest itself.' Bonehill's eyes blazed with triumph. 'I didn't want Carlos having any influence on you. Besides, he could no longer harm me.'

'But you must have known that Carlos would unleash the djinn,' Eliza gasped.

'Yes, but I knew Ness would kill the djinn, even if the bottle were opened,' Bonehill bragged.

'How could you know that?' Eliza hissed. 'The djinn cursed you.'

'No, he cursed himself,' Bonehill laughed. 'He said, "The child that your wife so fervently wished for will kill its father." She's no child of mine. She has always been just what her name says – a necessity, a means to an end.'

Ness frowned from her foggy view of the world. A dull pain stabbed her heart.

'But you should love me, Father. The djinn promised . . .' Ness began but she couldn't find any more words.

'Love you?' Bonehill's eyes glinted. 'I do love you, Necessity. I love your power and soon it will be mine to command!'

People love for different reasons. The djinn was right.

'Please, Anthony, I beg you. Don't do this to Necessity,' Eliza cried, slipping slightly on the thin ledge below the cross.

'Pathetic,' Bonehill spat. 'Now, child, enter the stone. Become my minion.'

Ness stared deep into the gem; its fires warmed her aching heart. She thought it would be nice to hide in there, away from the world and all its troubles. To forget the others. To forget her sorrows and bathe in the heat of the gem. Never to be reminded that her father despised her . . .

The bloodstone pulsed. Shadows shifted in its depths almost as if others moved around in there. And could she hear voices calling from within? No, not calling – crying, begging for help.

'Ness, no!' Eliza screamed. 'Think for yourself! You don't need to go into the jewel, don't let him draw you in. *I* called you Necessity because I need you more than life itself!'

Bonehill lashed out, striking his wife's cheek, sending her sliding further down to the base of the cross. She clung to the edge, her legs dangling over.

'Look into the bloodstone, my child. You have already become smoke, now join the fires in the gem.' Bonehill began chanting and Ness could feel the stone draw her. 'The beautiful bloodstone. You remember it, don't you?'

Ness shook her head, trying to resist, but it was like being pulled by a strong river current. The stone frightened her. She tried to block the pleading voices that howled from within. She looked down on the chaos below. Little people ran here and there, like thousands of tiny ants. Azuli lay, broken, on the roof below her. *Azuli!* Sorrow stabbed through her. She felt more solid, more awake, and yet still she hovered in the air. She glanced up beyond the glowing bloodstone at her father.

'You did this,' Ness spat. 'You planned it all. You caused the deaths of all these people.'

'What if I did?' Bonehill snarled. 'Only the strong survive, Ness. Didn't I always tell you that?'

'I'll not do your bidding, Father,' Ness hissed, starting towards him.

Bonehill shifted his position, still holding the cross with one hand. He lowered his boot on to his wife's fingers. 'You have no choice. Enter the bloodstone,' he said in a low voice, 'or your mother will have a nasty fall.'

Ness froze.

Her mother shook her head and gave her a warning glare. Ness made to cry out but it was too late. Eliza Bonehill wrapped her free arm around her husband's legs and pushed herself off the side.

It all happened so silently and slowly, it seemed. Ness watched as her mother and father, locked in a deadly embrace, struck the side of the lantern tower, rolled down the dome and took one final bounce before landing on the roof below.

Ness began to drift towards them, solidifying, moving faster as she took in what she had seen. Her heart pounded as she settled beside her mother, who lay on top of the shattered body of Anthony Bonehill.

'I always loved you, Ness,' she whispered. 'You know that, don't you?'

Ness nodded, mute and shaking, as she stared at her mother. Even bruised and grazed by the fall, she looked beautiful to Ness.

'I never meant to . . .' Eliza screwed her eyes shut, fighting the pain of her injuries. 'All I ever wanted was to protect you.'

'I know, Mama.' Ness gave a gentle smile and lowered her face to her mother's.

'I need . . . three wishes,' Eliza whispered. 'Wish number one,' she gasped. 'That Carlos Grossford had wished the djinn dead as he was meant to.'

Ness nodded and felt the magic welling up in her very core.

'Wish number two,' Eliza whispered. 'That Anthony Bonehill and Carlos Grossford had killed each other.'

'Mama, that's an evil wish. You can't –'

'Can't I?' Eliza gave a hard smile and coughed. Blood coated her lips. 'That is my wish. Trust me, Necessity.'

'And your third?' Ness sobbed.

'That once my other two wishes are completed, you are a djinn no longer but a normal, human young lady,' Eliza gasped, every breath rattling in her chest.

Ness hugged her mother close. 'Whatever you want, Mama.' She tried to smile through the tears. 'On one condition – we never forget who we were.'

Eliza nodded and the air seemed to shimmer. Ness's heart lurched as her mother, her father's broken corpse, the cathedral, the whole of London broke into numberless tiny fragments. All reality shattered and swirled around her as Ness felt the magic drain from her body and change everything, according to her mother's wishes.

Don't call a man fortunate until he's safely buried.

Traditional proverb

CHAPTER THIRTY-ONE
CHANGING

Ness was a cloud of smoke again, drifting over a different London. She drifted past Scrabsnitch's ramshackle shop, peeling its paintwork like a snake shedding skin, the dusty glass windows scarred with cracks; not the shining emporium she knew. Not yet.

She floated on over chimneys and slate rooftops then down into a tenement. Down into a cellar lined with green algae and cracked bones. Seven adults squeezed themselves into the putrid cell. Ness knew them all. Her mother and Scrabsnitch stood behind Widow Quilfy and Reverend Cullwirthy; Henry Lumm's wide frame hemmed the four of them against the wall. Next to him stood her father, his sneering face showing the world exactly what he thought of Grossford, who cowered on the floor.

There in the centre, surrounded by scattered bones and slime, sat Zaakiel.

Ness bit her lip. He looked strong, powerful.

'Remember what we agreed, Grossford,' Bonehill muttered. 'Don't worry, we'll take care of you.'

'What's this, Carlos?' the creature said, tilting his head. He had no nose to speak of, just two slits that expanded and contracted every now and then. His pointed chin ended in a wispy beard of wiry, black hair. Sores and boils wept from his parchment-like skin. 'A conspiracy?'

'Do it,' Bonehill snapped. 'Now.'

'I wish . . .' Grossford's voice became a hoarse whine. 'I . . . I . . . wish . . .'

'For God's sake, man, pull yourself together,' Bonehill cried.

'I wish that you were dead,' Grossford sobbed, running his words together. 'Now. This instant. Without doing another thing.'

The djinn's thin eyebrows rose, wrinkling his brow. He heaved a long, heavy sigh.

'Thank you,' he whispered, falling forward. 'After three thousand years of selfish, twisted, sickening wishes, this is the one wish I would have made for myself.'

Zaakiel gave a gasp and clutched his throat. Slowly, a sliver of blue light grew between his eyelids, widening and growing until the dazzling flare of his eyes expanded, consuming his head, neck and shoulders. Only Ness could watch; the others in the cellar cowered and covered their eyes against the blinding light. Zaakiel made no scream or howl of pain.

With a final brilliant flash, he vanished, leaving a smouldering black shadow on the ground and silence, apart from the sobbing of Widow Quilfy.

The Seven barely moved, still dazzled, recovering their vision in the dim cellar.

Then Ness was floating again, drifting, being pulled towards her mother's second wish. The rooftops of London spread out before her again and time seemed to rush forward. Fogs rolled up from the Thames with incredible speed; its waters rose and fell like some creature breathing; snow tumbled and melted quickly as the years passed with speed.

New memories grew inside Ness: Christmases with her mother, a governess at home, dancing, laughter. She smiled as the new reality began to form.

But then it stopped, as if someone had snagged a leash and pulled Ness back from the new-found happiness. Ness stood in the shadows by the banks of the Thames. The moon shone through the latticework of scaffolding and rigging that formed this building site, reflected in the puddles of rank river water that lay in the rutted mud.

Two figures faced each other at the edge of the half-finished Thames embankment. Ness could see her father gripping Uncle Carlos's lapels. Carlos grinned drunkenly, his skin grey under the stubbly chin.

'Damn you, Grossford. Haven't you had enough already?' Bonehill hissed.

'Enough?' Grossford slurred. 'I've only just begun. You said you'd take care of me. I made the last wish. Remember what you promised!'

'But every time we pay you off, you come back for more,' Bonehill snarled. 'I've lost count of the times I've had to buy you out of jail or grease the palm of some ne'er-do-well who beat you at cards. You can't afford to carry on like this and neither can we.'

'I can do what I please.' Grossford grabbed hold of Bonehill's arms. Ness noticed the shabbiness of his jacket, the stains and frayed cuffs. 'You owe me.'

'No,' Bonehill said quite calmly. 'Enough is enough. Tonight is your last payment from us. If you come sniffing around Bonehill House again, I'll have you thrown into the street.'

Grossford gave a throaty chuckle. 'You don't scare me, Anthony. I remember you when you were nothing. A worthless army officer with debts as big as mine. Not any more. You parade around town with your carriages and airs and graces. Quite the family man too. Tell me, how is little Necessity?'

Ness gave a gasp. It sounded so strange to hear them talk about her as if she weren't there.

'Leave her out of this, Grossford,' Bonehill snapped, shaking him by his lapels.

'She is well, I trust?' Grossford grinned.

'I'm warning you.' Bonehill's voice was low now.

'I only ask because it would be a shame if any harm befell her,' Grossford said, smiling innocently. Sweat trickled down his forehead.

'No one threatens my family,' Bonehill said, his eyes wide with rage. He shook himself free of Grossford and gave him a sharp push.

With a yell, Grossford fell back. For a second, he

seemed poised, leaning ridiculously far back over the edge, his arms spinning as he tried to regain his balance.

Ness stared in horror as, in that moment, he flicked his hands forward and gripped Bonehill's collar. Together they disappeared over the side of the embankment. Ness squeezed her eyes shut at the distant splash from the black Thames water below.

'Father!' Ness yelled, trying to run to him.

But the edge seemed further and further away. She felt so weak that the slightest breeze from the river blew her back. Tears coursed down her cheeks and time rolled further on.

More scenes played out before Ness. Policemen huddled around a shadowy form on the riverside. Her mother standing tall and gaunt at the funeral. Ness saw Lumm alive and well, staring pompously at her mother as they shook hands over the grave.

The Reverend Cullwirthy slipped between the headstones towards her. Ness could feel her neck prickle as the man drew nearer in his vestments and black cloth. *Hypocrite*, she thought. *He's lucky to be alive!* She shivered at the memory of his hideous transformation.

'Mrs Bonehill,' he said, giving Eliza's hand a gentle shake. 'My condolences in this time of sadness. If there's anything more I can do . . .'

'Yes,' Eliza said. 'There is.'

'Madam, just say the word,' Cullwirthy replied, licking his lips and smoothing his lank brown hair back.

'You can scurry back down whatever hole you were in

when my husband found you and never darken my door again. Do I make myself clear? I allowed you to conduct this service to keep up appearances. You were a friend of my husband's inasmuch as he had any friends at all, but now he has gone you will never be welcome at my house.'

Cullwirthy gave a curt nod and stamped off across the graveyard to the church. Ness grinned. She wanted to hug her mother but still time rolled on.

As she drifted higher up across the ever-changing London skyline, she watched buildings come down, other buildings rise and the embankment grow.

The pain of her father's death faded. Newer memories began to form in her mind again. Uncles and aunts she'd never met before, driven away by Anthony Bonehill's arrogance, now lavished love and gifts upon her. She saw herself singing at a piano, riding a pony with cousins she'd never known she had. Her mother's laughter rang freely around Bonehill House and Rowson the butler went smiling about his duties. A rather strict but fair governess lurked in the corners of the house and Ness realised that she never had to return to Rookery Heights. In fact, she'd never attended the Academy. She knew Sarah, Mollie and Hannah were all fit and well somewhere. *So is Miss Pinchett*, Ness thought, *but you can't have everything.*

Ness smiled and closed her eyes, revelling in this new happiness. A warm drowsiness crept over her and she melted into a delicious dreamless sleep.

*

The creaking of her bedroom door and the smell of toast tickling her nose woke Ness. She found herself lying in a bed. Her bed. In her room. Two sets of memories jostled in her head but somehow the djinn and the Pestilents seemed more like a vivid unpleasant dream. Ness smiled and looked up at her mother, who carried breakfast in on a tray.

'You slept late, Necessity.' Eliza smiled, setting the tray on to Ness's lap once she had sat up in bed. 'I thought I'd bring this up myself. Rowson pulled quite a face.'

Ness smiled. 'He's such an old woman sometimes!'

'You'd better hurry up though,' Eliza said, clapping her hands excitedly. 'Evenyule is visiting this morning. Apparently he's bringing some of your father's belongings that were cluttering up his shop. Sergeant Major Morris is just getting the carriage ready.'

'Sergeant Major Morris?' Ness grinned. An image of Morris in smart footman's livery popped into her memory. 'Of course!'

Eliza stared deep into Ness's eyes and, for a moment, they shared the secret knowledge of the other reality that never was. Ness frowned.

'What troubles you, Ness?' Eliza said, smiling gently.

'Your wishes,' Ness murmured. 'Why didn't you wish for the djinn never to have been found?'

'Because if the djinn had never been found, I would never have had you, my love,' Eliza said, settling on the end of the bed.

Ness returned her mother's smile but she noticed a glint of sadness in her eye. With her mother's choice of wishes, Father's wish remained and Ness's grandparents had still died in the freak carriage accident.

'But why did Father and Uncle Carlos have to die?' Ness said in a small voice.

'They knew about you and would never have left you alone,' Eliza sighed. 'You would have had no peace while either of those men lived. Anthony would have killed you in his lust for power, especially after my third wish. I had to wish them dead.'

'But you wished I was human and not a djinn,' Ness said. 'Father would have had no reason to harm me.'

'Believe me, Necessity, your father would have stopped at nothing to achieve his dream of controlling a djinn,' Eliza said, her voice thick with emotion. 'I can't bear to think what he would have put you through in some insane attempt to reverse the wish. Now, will you answer one of my questions?'

'All right.' Ness looked nervously at her mother.

'Your one condition. Why did you still want to remember everything that happened?' Eliza said, tilting her head. 'We could have lived in blissful ignorance.'

Ness felt her cheeks flush. 'Because I've changed,' she muttered, looking down. 'I didn't want to be who I was before.'

'I don't understand.' Eliza frowned and ran a finger through Ness's thick black hair.

'I was horrible before all this – cruel, a bully.' Ness's voice dropped to a whisper. 'Like Father. Besides, there was someone I didn't want to forget.'

'Someone?' Eliza gave a smile. 'Come on, you can tell me.'

Ness froze, holding her toast somewhere between mouth and plate, and stared at her mother. 'The Lashkars,' she whispered finally. 'Could it be?'

'Pardon?' Eliza said, still smiling. 'Ness, you aren't making any sense.'

But Necessity Bonehill jumped out of her bed, sending her breakfast tray clattering across the covers, and ran downstairs to her father's study.

She who can wait obtains what she wishes.

Traditional proverb

EPILOGUE

Ness gripped the front of the carpet, skimming it over the rooftops, veering round chimney pots at the last moment and whooping through arches. The folk below looked up but few were fast enough to see anything and those that did refused to believe their eyes. It was a chill morning but her thick scarf kept her warm. *If Mama hadn't wished for me to be an ordinary human girl, then I could fly myself.* She grinned. *But I like it better this way.*

One hand kept a firm grip on the carpet, the other clutched the precious object in her palm. She slowed the carpet down, taking in the alleyways and trying to remember the route as she skimmed towards the alcove that held the secret gateway to Arabesque Alley.

What if they've moved on? Ness thought. *There's no djinn, so there's no reason for them to stay in London.* Perhaps the Alley wouldn't be there, just crumbling slums. But Ness soon saw the alcove and found herself gazing down on a familiar busy square.

The weak morning sun shimmered on the water in the fountain at the centre and reflected off the white-washed buildings, making the whole place appear bright. The blue shutters were closed against the chill mist that persisted from the dawn.

The Lashkars shuffled around from stall to stall, carrying baskets and bales on their backs or heads. A lone figure sat at the fountain's edge, shoulders slumped.

Azuli! Ness's heart leapt. Without thinking, she swept down on the carpet and landed in front of him. The crowd cried out. An old woman screamed and stumbled back into one of the stalls, sending fruit rolling across the cobbles in all directions.

'What on earth?' Azuli jumped up, dragging his scimitar from his belt. He swung the blade in a deadly arc, barely giving Ness a chance to throw herself backward.

'Azuli!' Ness cried. 'It's me, you stupid boy!'

'You know my name! What enchantment is this?' Azuli demanded. 'And who are you calling stupid?' He thrust again at Ness, who leapt aside easily.

'It's no enchantment,' Ness began. 'Well, it is, but . . .'

The inhabitants of Arabesque Alley gathered around, eyeing Ness warily.

'A-ha!' Azuli snarled. 'What are you, some kind of djinn? Well, you've come to the wrong place. I am a Lashkar of Sulayman, skilled in fighting the powers of evil.'

'I'm not a djinn,' Ness said, ducking another swipe. 'Now hear me out or I'll have to take that sword from you.'

People began to run off. Someone called Hafid's name.

'Ha! No man or woman has bested Azuli of the Lashkars of Sulayman yet,' Azuli said, puffing his chest out.

'Only because you've never actually fought anyone,' Ness replied, blocking his sword arm and kicking his legs from under him.

'Stop this at once!' a voice cried from behind Ness.

She turned to see Jabalah and Taimur pushing through the crowd, followed closely by Hafid.

'Azuli! What is going on?' Taimur barked. 'What are you doing brawling in the square with a . . .' He stopped and stared open-mouthed at Ness. 'A girl?'

Azuli scrambled to his feet, glaring at Ness and dusting himself down.

'I wondered how long it would take you to find us again, Necessity Bonehill,' Hafid said, smiling.

'You know me?' Ness stared at the old man. 'You . . . you remember?'

'I have a little ancient wisdom,' Hafid said. 'I can still see things that might have been, or have been and have . . . changed.' Hafid flicked a frown towards Azuli. 'Is he being difficult?'

'Nothing I can't handle.' Ness beamed, taking a step towards Azuli.

'Hafid,' Jabalah said, scratching his head, 'what are you talking about? Do you know this young lady?'

'You may come to understand in time,' Hafid said, giving an enigmatic smile. 'For now, believe me when I say that Miss Necessity Bonehill is our honoured guest and should be treated accordingly.'

Jabalah exchanged glances with Taimur and then bowed low to Ness.

'Miss Bonehill,' Jabalah said, taking her hand, 'it's an honour to meet you.'

'Thank you, Jabalah.' Ness smiled mischievously at the man's startled face.

'How does she know my name?' Jabalah stuttered.

'Charmed, I am sure.' Taimur gave a curt nod and folded his arms. 'Wait a moment. Bonehill? Are you Anthony Bonehill's daughter?'

'She is nothing like her late father, Taimur,' Hafid said, calming the gaunt warrior. 'Besides, whatever you think of them, we owe the Bonehills a debt of gratitude for destroying the last djinn.'

'You know about that?' Ness said, surprised.

'The last sword melted away soon after Grossford wished Zaakiel dead,' Hafid said, smiling. 'It took but a few free drinks to verify the truth from Carlos.'

'I'll give you the benefit of the doubt,' Taimur muttered, glaring at Ness. 'But I still want to know why you knocked my son over.'

'She took me by surprise, Father, on that carpet,' Azuli gabbled. 'She flew out of the sky!'

Ness rolled the carpet up and hugged it close.

'Enough of this,' Hafid said, holding a bony hand up.

'I am pleased to see you, Necessity, but what brings you to our humble marketplace?'

'This ring,' Ness murmured and opened her hand to reveal the bloodstone. 'I awoke this morning and remembered it.'

'Remembered?' Hafid repeated. 'What did you remember?'

Ness drew Hafid aside. 'When my father tried to draw me into the bloodstone,' Ness whispered, 'I heard voices crying for help from within.'

Hafid's wizened face paled. 'Could it be?' he hissed. 'Where did your father come by this ring?'

'I'm not sure,' Ness admitted. 'He was very secretive about such matters but he discovered it some ten years ago.'

'The Lashkars were cursed by the djinn Amoteth ten years ago,' Hafid said, his voice barely audible. 'Could they have been trapped in the same stone?'

'How do we open it?' Ness stammered, feverishly running a finger over the stone.

'It just needs breaking,' Hafid said. 'A simple sword blow would suffice.'

He took the ring with trembling fingers and placed it on the edge of the fountain.

Jabalah stepped forward. 'Hafid,' he said, his face creased with concern, 'what are you doing?'

'You'll see, Jabalah,' Hafid said, smiling. 'Strike that ring. Hit the jewel with all your might.'

'But –'

'Just humour me,' Hafid said, raising his hand. 'Please, strike it with your sword.'

Sensing possible danger, the people of Arabesque Alley shuffled back to the edges of the market square. Jabalah glanced over to Taimur then unsheathed his sword.

Ness could barely watch as Jabalah raised his scimitar above his head and paused for a second. The air whistled as the butcher's blade sliced down on the ring. Jabalah gave a yell as metal struck stone with a loud *clang*. The sword grated down on the side of the fountain and the ring whirled off across the square with a metallic *ping*.

There was silence. It seemed everyone in the square sensed something was about to happen and was holding their breath.

Thin tendrils of red smoke began to emanate from the cracked jewel. The smoke thickened and became a red mist that filled the square so that Ness couldn't see more than an arm's length in front of her. People coughed and spluttered around her, vague phantom shapes in the blood-red fog.

Gradually the red cloud thinned to a pink haze. Ness frowned. The square seemed fuller. There were more Lashkars than before. Her heart leapt.

There in the centre of the square, standing bewildered, dusting themselves down, glancing at one another, stood a huge congregation of young men, women and children dressed in the same style as Hafid and his kin.

The old Lashkars stared in mute disbelief at their returned children. And then pandemonium broke out as both sides ran to greet each other. Father met son, mother ran to daughter. Tears flowed freely as children were raised up and hugged for dear life. Ness saw Jabalah and Suha with their arms wrapped around a young man she recognised from the portrait in their house. Hafid moved among the riot, grinning and shaking hands.

Tears stained Ness's cheeks as she watched the reunion. Only Azuli stood unmoved, arms folded, watching the joyous reunion apart. He watched Taimur as he steered a young girl towards him.

'His real daughter,' Azuli murmured to Ness. 'He won't have any time for me now.'

But Taimur gathered Azuli and his daughter in his arms and hugged them together.

'This is your brother,' he said to the little girl.

The girl beamed up at Azuli.

'Just remember, I'm the eldest so I'm in charge!' Azuli said, narrowing his eyes at the girl but squeezing out a smile too.

The celebrations seemed to last all day. Tables appeared from within houses and goods on the market stalls found their way on to the tables, given with a free heart. Ness sat watching as music played and people danced. Braziers were lit as the evening closed in and still the Lashkars sat and talked and drank and ate together.

Ness watched as the years of separation within the families seemed to melt away. Children played in the passages and across the square, and Arabesque Alley was full of life. She watched as Hafid hobbled his way through the crowd towards her and sat down with a sigh.

'We can never thank you enough, Necessity,' the old man said with a smile.

'I'm glad I could help,' Ness muttered, blushing.

Hafid's smile dropped for a moment. 'You will always be counted as one of our number, Necessity Bonehill,' he said, his voice shaking with emotion. 'If you ever need our help or food or shelter you only have to ask and it will be yours.'

Ness swallowed back a tear. 'Thank you, Hafid,' she stammered. 'That's a great honour. And what will you do now the last of the djinns has gone?'

Hafid shook his head. 'Who knows? Maybe one day we'll move away from this cold country and return to the land of our forefathers. For now we seek other means of employment here.'

'What do you mean?' Ness said, frowning.

'The Lashkars are skilled warriors,' Hafid said, 'experienced in fighting threats that are more, shall we say, unnatural.'

'Is there a need for such services?' Ness asked.

'What do you think?' Hafid stared blindly into the shadows.

Ness thought of all she had experienced: the djinn, the bloodsuckers, the Pestilents, not to mention her father. She nodded.

Azuli appeared, his eyes wide. Not far behind him, his sister, giggling, waved a broom over her head. 'Help me,' he cried. 'The girl is a demon. She will kill me before the night is through!'

'I think he needs rescuing.' Hafid grinned.

'I do too,' Ness said, smiling back.

She unrolled the carpet and climbed on. Bidding Hafid goodnight, she swooped after Azuli, flitting over his sister's head and scooping him up on to the carpet. It bucked and flickered against the new weight but kept level.

'What are you doing?' Azuli yelled. 'I should have pinned you down when I had the chance.'

'You never had the chance. I should have knocked you out,' Ness said. 'Arrogance is a terrible quality in a person. Believe me, I know.'

'Me, arrogant?' Azuli said. 'Hafid, help! This mad girl is kidnapping me!'

Ness grinned and steered the carpet up towards the full moon. All she had to do was teach this boy a few lessons in humility. And time was on her side now.

Turn the page for a spine-tingling bonus story!

Mr Grimhurst's Treasure

London, 1855

Josie stood glowering at Alfie, her arms folded. The moonlight shone brightly through the embalming room window, making everything stark and tinging it blue. The body had been brought in earlier that day. An old man, well-dressed. Fallen down the stairs, apparently.

'I don't know what yer worryin' about,' Alfie muttered, scratching his short-cropped blond hair. 'I'm just goin' to ask 'im a few questions.'

'I thought you weren't going to do this again,' Josie replied, flicking her hair over her shoulder indignantly. 'It seems to me that ever since the incident with Lord Corvis, you've been resurrecting more things, not fewer.'

'Look, this cove actually asked me to wake 'im up,' Alfie said, holding his hands out.

'Don't try and act all innocent – it makes you look like a frog,' Josie snapped, narrowing her eyes at him. 'Anyway, what d'you mean he asked you?'

'Found this on 'im, addressed to me!' Alfie said, pulling a piece of paper from his waistcoat pocket. Josie snatched it away. She unfolded the note and read it aloud.

Dear Master Alfie,

I write to you with a strange request but it is under the direst circumstances that I impose such a burden upon you. Should I, by some misfortune beyond my control, end up on your mortuary slab, I would ask a favour.

Rumour is a terrible thing, I know, but I was an acquaintance of Sebastian Mortlock's and so am open to the possibility that death is not the end. Within the circles I move I have heard talk that you may have certain 'abilities'. Should this be the case, I would implore you to awaken me just once if my mortal remains end up in your tender care.

Yours respectfully,
Horace Grimhurst

Josie frowned at the letter. 'If he moved in the same circles as Mortlock then he probably wasn't the most desirable individual,' she murmured. 'Why would he want to be awoken?'

'See, you wanna know too.' Alfie grinned. 'Well, I've done a bit of snoopin'. Horace Grimhurst wasn't a nice chap. I mean, not speakin' ill o' the dead an' all that, but he was a shocker!'

'A shocker?' Josie looked down at Mr Grimhurst. He looked sad with his grey face and silver hair, but the dead always looked a little pathetic to her. All their grand clothes, bows, ribbons and fancy haircuts counted for nothing once they lay on that table. 'In what way?'

'He was mean and cruel,' Alfie said. 'A terrible miser. Never gave anything to charity. Went through a whole load of wives.'

'Met his match with the last one though,' Josie said with a smirk. A hatchet-faced old woman who looked like sour milk had been smeared under her nose, Mrs Grimhurst had come in with her husband's body. 'Can't bear to have him in the house,' she had said, ruffling her black mourning silks. 'The sooner he's underground the better.'

'So what does he want with us?' Alfie raised an eyebrow, challenging Josie.

'Go on then,' Josie said and pursed her lips. 'But I don't like it.'

'Don't worry.' Alfie winked. 'Nothin' to it.'

Josie frowned. Was this the same boy she'd first met in this very embalming room only months ago? The boy who was terrified of his power? Now he seemed so accepting of these abilities that he almost revelled in them.

Alfie splayed his hand over the body of Horace Grimhurst and closed his eyes. His fingers began to tremble.

'Horace?' Alfie whispered. 'You there?' Alfie's body began to shake gently and he let out a long, rattling breath which was taken up by the corpse that lay before them. His shoulders jerked up from the table, making the head tilt back and the mouth swing open, but Horace Grimhurst's eyes stayed tight shut.

'*I . . . am . . . here*,' Grimhurst hissed. '*Thank . . . you*.'

'Why did you ask me to summon you, Mr Grimhurst?' Alfie said, his voice hoarse. Josie stared in horror as the corpse gave a gargling sigh. A tear stung her eye as she remembered the dark night when Alfie had awoken the Great Cardamom, her guardian. She could still see his bloody, eyeless sockets and the crimson tears that had trickled down his grey cheeks. She stared at her boots.

'*I . . . was . . . murdered*,' Grimhurst croaked.

Josie snapped her head up. 'What?' she gasped.

'*Mrs Grimhurst . . . pushed me . . . down the stairs*,' the corpse said. '*She wants . . . my money . . . but . . . you . . . can . . . have it*.'

'That's very generous, Mr Grimhurst, but –' Josie began, horrified.

'*She mustn't . . . benefit . . . from my murder*.' Grimhurst's voice became clearer, more assertive. '*You can . . . give the money to charity . . . I don't care . . . any . . . more*.'

'Where is it?' Alfie said, sweat trickling down his brow.

'*Most . . . of my wealth . . . is in gold coin*,' hissed Grimhurst. '*In a secret chamber . . . in the wine cellar*.'

'But we can't –' Josie started again.

'*Remove . . . the third bottle of port from the left . . . on the bottom row . . .*,' Grimhurst's lips barely moved, '*. . . and place it on the . . . first available space on the top row.*'

'Third from left on the bottom row,' Alfie repeated. 'First on top row.'

'Alfie, surely you're not thinking –' Josie stuttered.

'*This will open . . . a compartment behind . . . the bottle of port five spaces to the left . . . on the bottom row.*' Grimhurst's face twisted and grimaced as he spoke. '*Put this bottle . . . in the third space and take the gold . . . but do not replace the original bottle.*'

'But won't someone notice?' Alfie frowned, shaking with the effort of thinking and keeping Grimhurst awake.

'*I . . . hope so.*' The corpse gave a ghastly chuckle. '*Then . . . she'll know. Promise me . . . you'll . . . do this . . . Alfie . . .*'

'Yeah, I promise,' Alfie murmured.

'Alfie, no!' Josie gasped. 'You can't!'

But Alfie had slumped to the floor, exhausted after using his powers, and Mr Grimhurst was back in another place.

Throughout the day following Alfie's promise to steal Mr Grimhurst's treasure, Josie kept tight-lipped, refusing to talk to him. An icy silence stopped any conversation at the dinner table. But then Mr Wiggins spoke up, making Josie choke on her cup of tea.

'I have to pay a visit to Widow Grimhurst this evening to finalise the arrangements for her husband's funeral,' he said, standing at the table as if he were addressing a meeting of the Most Worshipful Order of Undertakers.

'Can we come, Mr Wiggins?' Alfie chirped straight away. 'I learn so much watchin' your way with the customers, like.'

Wiggins gave a proud smile. 'Why, of course, young Alfie. I was going to suggest such a thing myself. And what about you, Josie?'

'Very well,' Josie muttered. *At least then I can keep an eye on Alfie*, she thought.

Now the three of them walked briskly through the thick mist that shrouded the London streets. The grey fog of a freezing January evening created haloes around the yellow gaslights that dotted this well-heeled part of the city.

Josie dragged Alfie back from Mr Wiggins. 'You can't be serious about this, Alfie. If you get caught you could be put in jail,' she hissed. 'Mr Wiggins could be implicated too!'

'Make sure I'm not caught then.' Alfie grinned. However, his face became sober as he nodded over at Wiggins. 'Look at 'im, Josie. He ain't gettin' any younger an' what's he got to show for it? Business ain't what it was, an' so many younger chaps are gettin' into the undertakin' trade that old Wiggins barely makes a livin'.'

'I know,' Josie sighed. It was true. Times were hard and any ne'er-do-well from the Seven Dials could traipse up to Wiggins's Funeral Parlour with a sob story guaranteed to earn them a cheap funeral for their loved one. Josie had seen Wiggins forgo supper to pay for the hire of black horses so as not to pass the cost on to poorer customers. It was madness.

'Think what we could do with that treasure,' Alfie said. 'Mr Grimhurst wants us to 'ave it!'

'But –'

'All you 'ave to do is distract Mrs Grimhurst an' I'll slip downstairs,' Alfie whispered. 'It won't take a minute an' then we'll be rich.'

'Here we are,' Wiggins called to them as he mounted the steps to the Grimhursts' front door.

Mrs Grimhurst herself answered the door. 'We don't keep servants if we can do the work ourselves,' she observed, indicating that they should hang their coats up on the coat stand.

She was every bit as forbidding as Josie remembered. A bonnet of black silk emphasised her long face. Her thin mouth betrayed no emotion. She reminded Josie of Aunt Mag, tall and predatory as she stared down at them.

'Nothing fancy,' she said. 'Horace didn't set any money aside for fripperies and fancies. A grave, a box and a parson will be sufficient.'

'Are you all right, Josie?' Alfie suddenly piped up.

Startled, Josie glanced around. 'Who, me?' she said.

'Yeah, you look a bit . . . peaky,' Alfie murmured, squinting at her. 'Want me to get you a drink of water? Would you mind, Mrs Grimhurst?'

Mrs Grimhurst peered at Josie and snorted. 'She certainly looks a shade pale. Girls these days – no stamina.'

'Come on, Josie,' Alfie said, pulling her by the elbow. 'Let's get you a drink.'

'What are you playing at?' Josie hissed, once they were outside the room. 'I didn't say that I'd go along with this!'

Alfie winked. 'Yeah, well, you didn't say you wouldn't neither. C'mon, it's so simple. There's no servants.'

They hurried across the hall and down the stairs to the kitchen and cellars. The wine cellar proved easy to find. Alfie picked up an oil lamp from the kitchen table and led Josie down a short staircase.

'I'd forgotten how much I hate cellars,' he said, shuddering, 'after that business with the ghul in Corvis's mansion.'

Josie edged closer to Alfie. She too hadn't forgotten the creatures writhing about in the shadows of Rookery Heights. 'There's the wine rack,' she whispered, pointing to a gloomy corner.

'Now, let me see,' Alfie murmured, passing the oil lamp to Josie. 'Third from left on the bottom, then first on the top.' He picked out a dusty, greenish bottle and laid it on the top rack. 'Five spaces to the left on the bottom row,' he muttered to himself. 'Put this bottle in the third space and . . .'

A slight click echoed around the cellar.

'Very clever – must be all kinds of pulleys and levers behind this wall. 'Ere it is – the secret compartment,'

Alfie said as he slid his hand into the hole and pulled out a long, thin bag that hit the dusty floor with a satisfying *clink*.

He held up the bag with a victorious grin. Coins bulged through the material.

'I don't think you'll find a drink of water down here.' Widow Grimhurst's voice made Josie leap with fright. 'But I see you've found something of mine.' She held out her hand to receive the bag of gold, smirking triumphantly.

Mr Wiggins's bright red face appeared over the widow's shoulder. 'Josie? Alfie? What's going on? Why are you down here?'

'It seems these children have got themselves lost, Mr Wiggins,' Widow Grimhurst sneered. 'Either that or they've developed a taste for fine wine.'

Wiggins fidgeted from foot to foot, twisting his fingers around each other. 'Oh dear, this is so embarrassing. Please accept my apologies, Mrs Grimhurst. I don't know what's come over them.' Wiggins blustered on as the widow just stood there, weighing the bag in her hands, a sour grin on her face.

'I suppose young minds are apt to drift and they seem to have done me a favour.' She stared at Josie, then Alfie. 'I'll accept Mr Wiggins's plea on your behalf and won't call a constable. Now get out of my house.'

Widow Grimhurst almost skipped through the hall to the front door. Wiggins chased after her, gabbling apologetically.

'Please accept my apologies once again, Mrs Grimhurst.

They're good children really. They've been through rather a lot lately,' he chattered.

'Just make sure my odious husband is buried deep as soon as possible,' the widow muttered, 'and don't ever darken this door again.'

Josie and Alfie stumbled numbly down the front steps and into the street as the front door slammed shut. Josie just caught a glimpse of a triumphant leer on Mrs Grimhurst's craggy face and then Wiggins looked down at them, hands on hips.

'I don't know what to say,' he grumbled all the way home. 'Skulking around people's houses for no good reason! I've never been so ashamed. Not only have you let yourselves down but you've let me down too.'

Alfie sat silently in the embalming room, staring down at Horace Grimhurst's corpse. Josie shook her head.

'You should count yourself lucky,' she said. 'It could have been a lot worse.'

'Go on, say "I told you so" if it makes yer feel any better,' Alfie muttered. He raised a hand over the body.

'What are you playing at now?' Josie snapped.

'The least I can do is apologise,' Alfie growled. 'I promised 'im and I've failed. I'll have to make it right.'

Josie glared as Alfie began to shake. *Waking the dead is easier for him now. He's getting better at it*, she thought.

Horace Grimhurst suddenly lurched upright, his shoulders shaking. Josie stared, slack-jawed, as she realised that the corpse was laughing.

'Mr Grimhurst, I'm sorry,' Alfie said, downcast.

'*Sorry?*' chuckled Grimhurst. '*What . . . for?*'

'She found us with the gold and she's taken it,' Josie said, frowning. 'Why are you laughing?'

'*She's tried to . . . kill me . . . before . . . Several times.*' The cadaver shook with mirth. Alfie lifted up his head to listen. '*I wanted . . . her dead too. I kept a . . . bottle . . . of port . . . laced . . . with arsenic . . . ready.*'

'Oh Lord,' Alfie murmured. 'The one on the bottom row . . .'

'*I carried the . . . letter to you . . . in my . . . pocket . . . just in case . . . she got to me first.*' Grimhurst gave a rattling laugh. '*You . . . moved the poisoned bottle . . . up to the top. She'll be enjoying . . . her bedtime glass . . . just . . . about . . . now . . .*'

Josie and Alfie stared at each other in horror.

'*How I'm looking forward to . . . seeing her again . . . very soon.*' Horace Grimhurst gave a final gargling snigger and fell back, the breath sighing from his mouth.